The
MUCH BETTER
STORY BOOK

RED FOX

A Red Fox Book
Published by Random House Children's Books
20 Vauxhall Bridge Road, London SW1V 2SA

A division of Random House UK Ltd

London Melbourne Sydney Auckland
Johannesburg and agencies throughout the world

Red Fox and the Westminster Children's Hospital School would like to thank
JH Graphics for kindly typesetting this book free of charge, and Cox and Wyman
for printing the cover, also free of charge

Set in Baskerville
Typeset by JH Graphics Ltd, Reading

Printed and bound in Great Britain by
Cox & Wyman Ltd, Reading, Berkshire

ISBN 0 09 911531 X

Contents

5

SECTION 2 —
'The sun will chase your blues away' (Weather)

SECTION 3 —
'Lonely whale' (Green themes)

SECTION 4 —
'Beyond the rails' (Animals great and small)

SECTION 5 —
'Crunkle like a florncake' (Bits and bobs of nonsense)

SECTION 6 —
'They turn into people' (Other people)

SECTION 7 —
'A massive munch!' (Food)

SECTION 8 —
(Moving along) 'Fly to the moon'

SECTION 9 —
'Throw your head like a beachball' (It's magic)

Endpiece

Introduction

My dream

Last night I had a dream
The dream was sweet
The dream gave me so much pleasure
I wrote it down.
It became part of me
Each time I read it
My heart became warmer
It was so beautiful.
I wanted to dream it again
And looked for it in every dream
But I never saw it again

An extended period in hospital is a time when children experience new feelings, thoughts and impulses. Creative arts like music, dance, drama, poetry and literature encourage children to express their feelings, as the poem above illustrates perfectly. This was written by a fourteen-year-old girl with a life-threatening illness, who after a lengthy stay in hospital, found that poetry provided her with the perfect means for voicing her hopes, fears and feelings.

The Westminster Children's Hospital School offers children access to the Arts through workshops which are designed to be educational and healing by encouraging the acquisition of new skills and strengths while building on capacities and experience already possessed. The workshops also give the children a sense of working together in a stimulating, creative atmosphere.

The seeds of THE MUCH BETTER STORY BOOK were sown after some wonderful poetry was written during one of our workshops, and once the entries for our first story competition started to arrive. Children should have a sense that what they do can be seen and appreciated by people other than parents and teachers and our book has provided the perfect vehicle for this by combining the children's stories and poetry with generously contributed work by famous authors, poets and illustrators.

It has proved a difficult task to decide which children's stories and poems to include. Finally, after much heart searching, we chose the stories of the first prize winners from each age group, along with a mixture of poems. We are sorry that we couldn't find room for all our winners as the range and quality of the stories produced by our young authors was extremely impressive.

We have many people to thank for their part in the production of our book. In particular, Alison Berry, Publishing Director of RED FOX BOOKS, for her patience and advice, Caroline Thomas for her brilliant editing, Jennifer Curry for arranging the contents and Jane Asher for writing our foreword and for her continuing support of the hospital school. We would give enormous thanks to the authors and poets who have shared their skills by leading workshops which were attended by children who have a wide range of special needs thus capturing the children's imaginations and stimulating them to write proved an inspiration to us all. We also thank all the other contributors to our book who have been so generous with their time and talent.

And thank *you* for purchasing THE MUCH BETTER STORY BOOK and we hope all your family enjoy it. By doing so you have helped to support hospital education and in particular our own school. It is important to remember that all children in the community are potential hospital patients and so projects like this which involve schools and the wider community are vital if children in hospital are to have their special needs met and be given equal access to the full National Curriculum.

Now, as you turn the page, we welcome you to the world of words, wisdom and fantasy. Happy reading!

Janette Steele, M.A.
Headteacher.

and Joan Kingston,
Teacher and Events Organiser

FOR
CHILDREN IN HOSPITAL
ALL OVER THE WORLD

Foreword

by Jane Asher

A few years ago the beloved 18-month-old baby son of some good friends of mine was diagnosed as suffering from leukaemia. The skill, care and love he received at the Westminster Children's Hospital up to the moment of his tragic death have never been forgotten by any of us close to him. During the times I visited him and his mother I was impressed again and again not only by the dedication and efficiency shown towards the physical care of all the children in the hospital, but also by the close and caring attention paid to the other needs so often neglected in our technologically brilliant age. To ignore the insatiable demand of a child's mind for knowledge, stimulation and fantasy while curing his body is to tackle only half the problem.

In the Westminster Children's Hospital School this never happens. No child is allowed to feel isolated or bored; if he or she is unable to come to the school room then a teacher will go to the bedside. The level of skill and enthusiasm of the staff is remarkable, and I have seen many enthralled children whose idea of school will have been changed for the better forever thanks to their stay in the hospital.

This lovely book sums up all that is best in the

school's approach. A wonderful mixture of poems, stories and pictures by many eminent adult writers and illustrators and some talented young writers-to-be, it contains a cross section of jolly, sad and thoughtful ideas that will appeal to even the most glum of little readers, well or ill. By buying this book you are not only giving many hours of pleasure to the lucky child that reads or has read to them these stories and poems, but also directly supporting the vital work of the school. Every parent's nightmare is to see their child in pain and in hospital — this is a very special way of helping those for whom the nightmare has become a reality.

Prologue

The nurse she said

The nurse she said:
What you doing in bed?
I said: nothing.

The Matron came
And asked: What's your name?
I said: nobody.

The student with his comb
Said: Where's your home?
I said: nowhere.

The Doctor prodded,
The Doctor nodded.
I heard the Doctor say:
Who are you, anyway?
I said: nobody.

You see, I was feeling so miserable
That I was trying to turn inviserable.
Then they gave me a pill and a big mug of tea
And I floated away on a blackcurrant sea

And I don't know how it happened
But I know I was rapping
Yes flying over London
With my pyjamas flapping

Then I was hopping on the Moon
with my galactic Mum
Till I tripped on some Krypton
And landed on my bum.

And my eyes began to open
And I heard the Nurse say:
You've had your operation —
How are you today?
Nobody from Nowhere
Do you feel OK?

I'm not Nobody
From Nowhere, mate
I'm the Famous Somebody
And I feel great
And I just had a brilliant
Operation Dream
And so, by golly,
Better wheel me in a trolley
Full of starry pizza
Space jelly and moon ice cream.

*with love to all the children in
Westminster Hospital and the pupils
of Francis Holland School.
from Adrian Mitchell*

'Love Plus Luck' (Feelings)

Who's afraid of the dark?

I'm not afraid of the dark, not me —
Hang on, is that a flying bat I see?
A giant moth or a great black bird?
It's the curtain moving, don't be absurd!

What's that shape growing big and fat?
It's not a rhino, I'm sure of that!
A hippopotamus can't get through my door,
There are no snakes coiled on the floor.

I'm not afraid of the dark, not me —
I'm as brave as brave can be!
The creature climbing up the wall
Doesn't frighten me at all!

It can't be a spider huge and hairy,
Nor a green-eyed monster wild and scary.
It's not a lizard or a natterjack toad,
Just shadows of trees across the road.

I'm not afraid of the dark, not me —
But I wish Dad would bring my mug of tea!
When I hear his footsteps on the stair
My spooks all vanish into thin air.

I drink my tea and he gives me a hug
And there isn't a sign of beast or bug.
I close my eyes, drift off to sleep —
No ghosts to count, just white woolly sheep!

Moira Andrew

Lullaby *(For Nancy aged two)*

The house is silent.
Black-furred night is heaped against the window,
And one pale, luminous eye remarks
How slowly hours devour the light.
Sleep softly darling;
I shall keep three candles lit beside your bed,
Three golden blades will pierce the heart
Of night till morning finds him dead;
Sleep softly darling, sleep.

Vernon Scannell

Lucky sums

One plus one is two
And two plus two is four
When love plus luck plus you
Arrive at my front door.

But one from four leaves three
And three from four leaves one
While love from luck leaves me
Afraid you may not come.

Then two times four makes eight
And three times three makes nine
So love times luck times fate
Times you must equal MINE!

Two into ten goes five,
Five into ten goes two . . .
Oh I am the luckiest boy alive
Whose sums all end with you.

John Mole
Illustrated by Mary Rees

Huff

I am in a tremendous huff —
Really, really bad.
It isn't any ordinary huff —
It's one of the best I've had.

I plan to keep it up for a month
Or maybe for a year
And you needn't think you can make me smile
Or talk to you. No fear.

I can do without you and her and them —
Too late to make amends.
I'll think deep thoughts on my own for a while,
Then find some better friends.

And they'll be wise and kind and good
And bright enough to see
That they should behave with proper respect
Towards somebody like me.

I do like being in a huff —
Cold fury is so heady.
I've been like this for half an hour
And it's cheered me up already.

Perhaps I'll give them another chance,
Now I'm feeling stronger
But they'd better watch out — my next big huff
Could last much, much, much longer.

Wendy Cope

Mr Bigstuff

by Vyanne Samuels
Illustrated by Tony Ross

Mr Bigstuff had only one ambition in life and that was to be the biggest and the best of all the people that he came across. His motto in life was 'THE BIGGER THE BETTER THE BEST'.

He lived in a big house. It was the biggest house on the block. It had big windows, big doors and everything. In fact it was so big that it blocked the sun from everyone else's house. Mr Bigstuff wanted everyone to know how big and important his house was so he made sure that it got in the way of their sunshine.

Everything that Mr Bigstuff did was big.

His dog, Massive, was the biggest dog in the neighbourhood.

His car was the largest car on the road.

He grew the tallest rose bushes in the neighbourhood.

He even had the most gigantic garbage bin ever seen.

Unfortunately, not only was it the biggest bin, it was also the smelliest because the garbage men could not empty it.

As he had the biggest of everything for miles around, Mr Bigstuff felt that he was the most important person. His wife felt that she was the most important wife and his children felt that they were the most important children. Even Massive felt that he was the most important dog.

The Bigstuffs made sure that everyone saw how important they were by wearing what they thought were 'important' clothes. Mrs Bigstuff and her daughter Burletta wore huge hats, colossal collars, big bright blouses and shiny, shiny shoes. Mr Bigstuff and his son Barny also wore things that made them really stand out. When people stared at them, Mr Bigstuff thought that it was because they were the best, 'THE BIGGER THE BETTER THE BEST' Mr Bigstuff would say to himself with a big smile on his face.

There was a large property opposite Mr Bigstuff's house with a broken down old house on it. Mr Bigstuff did not pay it any mind as he could not see much of it through its thick, overgrown bushes. Besides, it was not blocking the rays of the sun from his house and, it was small.

One day, when the Bigstuffs were away on an extra long holiday, a lot of workmen went over to the small, broken down old house and started working on it.

'Over here!' shouted a carpenter to the truck driver who was delivering a large load of lumber to the little old house.

'OK, go for the next load!' said a plumber organizing his crew who were shifting yards of piping and fittings for the broken down old house. Builders, painters,

plumbers and carpenters came and went every day. Soon the broken down old house became a lovely little house.

Everyone in the neighbourhood came to admire the lovely little house. They all agreed that it was truly the best house in the neighbourhood. Then they all agreed that the new neighbours were the nicest family in the neighbourhood.

When the Bigstuffs returned from their long holiday and arrived at their home, they opened their eyes in amazement. 'Where did that house come from?!' they gasped looking across the road.

'It is even better than our house!' they exclaimed.

'I can't believe this!' Mr Bigstuff panicked.

'And right in front of our house.' said Mrs Bigstuff, still in shock.

Later that day, the Bigstuffs watched as an enormous truck with the word 'REMOVAL' printed on its long sides came slowly down the road. It stopped in front of the lovely little house. A car stopped behind it and the passengers got out. There were four of them. A man, a woman, two children and a dog.

'They look so ordinary!' huffed Burletta Bigstuff.

'Even the dog looks ordinary!' said her brother Barny.

Massive stopped panting as he watched the little corgi having a wonderful time digging for bones in his new yard. He looked down at his manicured claws wishing he could also dig for a bone and feel the soil on his paws just once.

The Bigstuffs watched the new family move in.

'Just take a look at that furniture — it's fabulous! Their carpets are magnificent, the paintings are beautiful, those enormous plants — incredible . . .' sighed Mrs Bigstuff looking around her house and comparing every little thing with whatever the removal men took into the little house across the street.

'And look at those wonderful toys — they've got everything!' shrieked Barny, unable to control his jealousy.

But Burletta was noticing how many people were going over there.

'No one ever comes over to our house. How come they're so important already?' she complained to herself and she walked off in disgust because she just could not stand it.

Mr Bigstuff meanwhile, was very quiet. He was thinking very hard. 'With these new people in the neighbourhood, with all the attention they're getting, their lovely things and lovely house, how can we be the most important?'

That night, Mr Bigstuff went to bed feeling quite ill. The words 'THE BIGGER THE BETTER THE BEST' kept haunting him. He had a nightmare where he shrank to the size of a mouse and no one noticed him as he was just too small and not important enough. But something did. Massive the dog noticed him. He spied Mr Bigstuff amongst the toys and ran over to pick up the tiny moving object with his sharp teeth which were wired with braces.

'No, Massive!' yelled Mr Bigstuff, 'Heel, boy! Heel!' he panicked. But it was no use. Massive kept coming. Mr Bigstuff looked around quickly for somewhere to hide. 'Yes!' he shouted when he saw his son's red toy fire engine. He jumped into the driver's seat and drove over to a nearby armchair. Then he ran up the escape ladder, jumped on to a cushion and bounced up to the back of the chair. Massive was sniffing around the chair, drooling and getting excited at the thought of chewing the tiny object, when he bumped into the chair sending Mr Bigstuff flying through the air. Mr Bigstuff was heading for the floor below Massive's shiny braces when he suddenly woke up out of his dream sweating.

'Huh?!' he exclaimed, trying to wake himself completely out of his sleep. But the words 'THE BIGGER THE BETTER THE BEST' were still haunting him even when he was awake.

The second that daylight appeared, he jumped up out of bed and looked through the window. 'It's still there,' he groaned as he closed back the curtains quickly so that he could no longer see the little house across the road.

'I have to get out of here, I know what I have to do,' he said to his reflection in the mirror. He had already spent a long time looking at himself to see if he had shrunk at all whilst asleep.

'What about your breakfast?' asked Mrs Bigstuff

when she realized that her husband had not even noticed the eggs, pancakes, bacon, fried fish, cereal, toast, and danish that she usually gave him for breakfast.

'Aren't you feeling well?' Mrs Bigstuff wondered.

'Yes. I mean no. What I mean is that I have to get out of here,' he replied and ran outside.

'But . . .' Mrs Bigstuff tried to stop him, but he had already driven off in his big-wheeled truck. 'I guess he's too important for people to laugh at him wearing his pyjamas,' she mumbled to herself, went inside and shut the door.

Mr Bigstuff stopped his truck at the hardware store. He took giant sized steps through the door and moments later came out beaming. The men from the hardware store loaded the goods on to the back of the truck and watched in bewilderment as Mr Bigstuff drove off at great speed.

'It's the first time that I've ever seen anyone buy that amount of that kind of glass!' said one store assistant to another.

'Mmm. Wonder what he's going to do with it?' said a third one thoughtfully.

Soon, the front of Mr Bigstuff's house was full of workmen cutting and removing, replacing and fixing the huge glass in the front of the house. By midday, there was a much thicker glass in every window pane of the Biggstuff's house. The workmen left looking back at the house in astonishment.

'Come! Come everybody!' Mr Bigstuff called out on his loud speaker to his family who were busy in all parts of the house.

They came running to the living room where they found him looking, smiling, through his new glass window.

Mrs Bigstuff, Burletta and Barny looked through the window and smiled too. They were all smiling at Mr Bigstuff's big idea. Even Massive looked as though he was smiling.

The new people across the road in the lovely little house were also looking out through their window. But they were not smiling. They could not believe their eyes. The Bigstuffs looked bigger than ever and everything inside the Bigstuff's house looked ten times bigger than before. Even their dog was bigger than ever. The new glass in the front window made everything look bigger than normal.

That afternoon, the rays of the sun beat down on Mr Bigstuff's house. Stronger and stronger they shone, making everything hotter and hotter. No one except the new neighbours across the road noticed how fierce the sun was shining, as Mr Bigstuff's house blocked everyone else's house from it. But the new neighbours noticed that the sun was shining brighter than ever on the Bigstuff's large front glass window. They also noticed that the rays of the sun on the glass window were dazzling. And then

they noticed that the oversized, overstuffed furniture in the house looked as though it was glowing. Then everything behind the glass started to smoke, then crackle, then burn. Suddenly, flames started to appear. The Bigstuffs ran around the house looking for something to put out the flames, but they were too late as everything was bursting into flames. Instead, they ran out of the house and into the street. The Bigstuffs watched as the gigantic flames swallowed everything inside their house. By the time the fire department put out the fire, and it was all over, not much more was left than a big pile of burnt things.

'Let that be a lesson to you sir,' said the fireman with a stern look on his face. 'You should never use magnifying glass anywhere that it comes into contact with the sun! Magnifying glass makes the sun's rays many times

stronger — makes stuff burn. Never use this kind of glass for this purpose again. If you do you're just asking for trouble — big trouble.'

Mr Bigstuff nodded his head in silence. He was thinking. 'Big trouble . . .'

But his thoughts were broken by Barny and Burletta. 'The bigger the better is not really the best you know, Dad,' they said.

'Those people over the road seemed more important than us to everybody, and they didn't have big stuff like we did,' said Burletta.

'Yes, even the new kid's skateboard is smaller than mine but he has more fun on it because it can go around corners and race with the other guys. Mine is so big that I can't steer it and all it does is knock everyone else's skateboard off the road,' said Barny.

Mrs Bigstuff just looked at her husband. The children had said it all.

Then the family saw him smiling at the pile of ashes. 'I have decided that being BIGGER is not always the best. Being ordinary can't be so bad!'

'Yes!' he went on, clicking his fingers in excitement, 'THE MORE ORDINARY THE BETTER.'

Mr Bigstuff set about making an ordinary house exactly where his big house had been. The family started to wear ordinary clothes and do ordinary things. Massive even had his braces removed. Soon the neighbours noticed that all of the big things that had been a nuisance to them had gone. It was not long before they all came around to visit and be friendly, and decided that the Bigstuffs were quite nice really.

So the family was happy, the neighbours were happy and even Massive was happy. Being ordinary was no big thing.

Fire

scarlet
spikes,
stinging
fingers

Fire
laughs
at
people's
pain.

Gary Boswell

Dunce

I always try my hardest,
I always do my best,
But I just don't seem to be,
As clever as the rest.

Anna Luscombe, aged 8
Francis Holland School
London

Presents

I got a hamster
I didn't exactly want one

I got a turtle tracksuit
It's not my style

I got an ashtray
It had my name on
But I don't smoke
I gave it to my grandad

I got a pair of trainers
Wrong size
But worst the wrong label

But what I really liked were the thoughts

James Street
Westminster Children's Hospital School
Illustrated by Satoshi Kitamura

'The sun will chase your blues away' (Weather)

The sun

The wind is whistling.
The sky is grey.
You're off to school
On a miserable day.

Clouds are pouring
Rain on your head.
You wish you could
Have stayed in bed.

But 92 million
Miles from here
Is a star that will make
Your gloom disappear.

Its rays will cross
The deeps of space
To make you smile
When they touch your face.

The sun will chase
Your blues away.
For who can be sad
On a bright, sunny day?

Tony Bradman
Illustrated by Satoshi Kitamura

The boy who wanted the sun

by Sadie Ann Twomey, aged 6
St Vincent de Paul School
3rd prize

The sun was shining in the window. Jeff said to his mummy 'I want the sun.'

'You won't get the sun in a shop' said his mummy.

Later that day, he was so silly that he tried to fly. It didn't work so he bounced up and down. He saw a helicopter on the ground. He didn't know how to fly it. He played around with it and at last it flew. It didn't go up to the sun.

Jeff found a rope and he made a very big loop. He thought he could throw it round the sun and that's what he did but he missed. He tried again and he got something but it slipped through and he saw that it was only a cloud. He thought he'd got the sun and he pulled it along behind the helicopter. When he landed he jumped out but there was no sun. It was still high in the sky.

34

At the Musée D'Art Naïf

At the bottom of a hill in Montmartre
where you look up to the church and
the crawling cable cars is a signpost
which directs you to the Musée d'Art Naïf.

Above it there is always a small halo
of blue sky or if it rains the rain falls
in straight rods of silver and the winds
blow around it in perfect circles of
whistling breath and nearby someone sings
through a window which is not quite closed.

There, if you walk in the direction the signpost shows, past small shops that look as though
they are used, saying Bonjour to the people
who use them, you are glad to be in Montmartre
in clean air looking for the Musée d'Art Naïf.

And you will find, where the rain stops and
there is a smell of sunshine, a small building
which is not labelled but has two galleries
of paintings and a well-behaved sheep which
baas quietly from a pen in the wet-scrubbed
foyer beside a turnstile, a tiny cafe and
a ticket lady with an early-morning face.

In the gallery d'Art Naïf the pictures are
arranged in countries and you can walk through
Europe spending an hour in Czechoslovakia.
And every portrait looks like someone
and there are families working in fields
or in farms among animals with familiar faces
and angels come and go in the Garden of Eden
where the sun shines in the middle of the sky
and you can see each leaf plainly on every tree.

And on certain weekdays a crocodile of children
invade the Musée d'Art Naïf to call the dozing
sheep awake and run among the portraits
and the animals and the angels coming and going
in the sunshine in the Garden of Eden.

And when they leave, the silence in the Musée
d'Art Naïf in the middle of Montmartre on an
ordinary morning is like the silence of the
world on the seventh day of Creation when
everything is astonished at what it has become.

Edwin Brock

Flamenco

Days dance into summer
wearing new green shoes
and yellow skirts, toes
tapping to tambourines
shaken in the treetops.

Moira Andrew

The problems of Mr and Mrs Brollytrouble

by Sophie Lewis, aged 10
St Christopher's School, Hampstead
London
2nd prize
Illustrated by David McKee

'Oh dear,' sighed Mr Brollytrouble, 'we don't have an umbrella or even a sunshade that hasn't got a missing spoke or a tear or a broken handle.'

'Well darling, we must get some unbroken umbrellas then,' replied Mrs Brollytrouble. 'Let me go out and buy some.'

'Hortensia! You will NOT go out and buy some. I remember the last time you "went out and bought" something or other. We must get rid of these terrible umbrellas first.'

So Mr and Mrs Brollytrouble, and Grandma and Grandad, and all the Aunties and Uncles, that were scattered over the world, that belonged to the Brollytroubles, including the two Brollytrouble daughters, tried their very best to lose the umbrellas. They left them on buses, in cinemas, in other people's dustbins and by accidentally dropping them into wet concrete. They even put them in boxes with false addresses on them and posted them, but, no matter how hard they tried, those umbrellas always found the way back.

'This is terrible,' groaned Mr Brollytrouble. 'The only thing to do is to have them made into other things. So they paid a jewellery company a hundred pounds to make 28 stainless steel brooches and another company to make 16 pairs of waterproof stockings.

Then they started gathering more *good* umbrellas: Mrs Brollytrouble won one, with long elegant tassels, for being the best at bridge (she wasn't really,but she blackmailed the other players into saying that she was). Mr Brollytrouble was given one, with a complicated handle, by his best friend. Both the Brollytroubles were presented, each with several different umbrellas,by an umbrella-making company to whom they had donated some money. Grandma was given one with a computer in the handle and a mechanism for measuring the force and number of the raindrops that dropped on it, for being the oldest female citizen in the town. Aunty Josephine sent twelve crisp packets off to receive an umbrella that changed colour according to the temperature of its handle. Uncle Patrick won second prize in an athletics competition and was awarded a gold umbrella as well as an accidentally picked up one, with a hollow handle in which you could put cigarettes!!!

Then the Brollytroubles threw a party inviting all their relations. On the night just before the party, each person secretly thought, 'I'll bring my new umbrella. It will be the best there and everyone will envy me.'

But when everyone was dancing, Mrs Brollytrouble slipped out of the room to look at all the umbrellas in the hall. She tried to pick up the gold umbrella when, being extremely heavy, it slid from her grasp and fell, breaking every other umbrella in the room at the same time.

'Oh no!' she gasped in dismay and as she said that the sky outside burst open and the rain poured down.

Rain

Rain can clatter from a gutter
Or sputter off a wall.
It can drip in single droplets
Or . . . not fall down at all.
It can sprinkle round in showers
Or come sloshing down for hours
It can dribble
It can drop
It can splish splash plop.
It can run in little trickles
Which sometimes tend to tickle
When they wriggle off your hair
And wet your neck all bare.
It can wash away big houses
Or drown sheep and farmers' cowses
It can burble
It can slop
It's been even known to stop —

Hugh Scott

Stig in the flood

by Clive King
Illustrated by Shirley Hughes

'It's going to be a lot of fun at Granny's if it rains all the time,' Lou sniffed.

Lou and her young brother Barney were going to stay with Granny. They were sitting in the big coach, looking at the rain which never seemed to stop.

'Perhaps we'll have a big flood,' Barney said hopefully.

There was a stopping place and three noisy boys got in, dripping wet. Lou nudged Barney. 'Aren't those your friends?' she whispered.

Barney looked round. Yes, they were the Snarget brothers, Norm, Ern and Arf. Last time he'd stayed at Granny's, he had met them in the Dump.

With Stig.

When Barney was away from West Yoke he could hardly believe in Stig, living there in his cave in the chalk pit. But he was looking forward to seeing Stig again. Stig was his friend. He wasn't so sure about the Snargets.

The Snargets crowded into the seat in front of Barney and Lou and hung over the back of it, chewing bubblegum.

'Look who's here!'

'It's old Barney!'

'Watcher, Barn! Watcher doing here?'

Barney said, 'I'm going to my Granny's.'

The Snargets said they'd been staying with their auntie on a farm, but now they were going home and they didn't want to.

'We don't seem to be going anywhere,' Lou said. The coach had gone only a little way from the last stop and now it was standing in a big puddle of water that went right across the road.

A white van with a blue light on top came steaming along towards them, sending up a big wave in front of it. A policeman leaned out of the window and shouted to the coach-driver.

'The river's over-flowed. There's no way through.' And the van went on.

The driver backed the big coach, turned round in a little lane, and drove back to the last stop.

When he got there he went along the coach and spoke to the people. He came to the Snargets.

'You boys got on here, didn't you? You better get off and stay here.'

'Hooray!' shouted the Snargets.

'What about you two?' the driver said to Barney and Lou. 'You've come a long way, haven't you? We'll have to get you back to your mum.'

'But she won't be there!' Lou said. 'She's going away herself.'

'That's OK, mister,' said the oldest Snarget cheerfully. 'They can stay at my auntie's with us.'

'You're all friends, are you?' said the driver, and moved on down the coach. Lou didn't look much happier, but Barney thought it might be fun to stay with the Snargets.

They all got out. Ern pointed through the rain to the car park.

'There's Auntie's car!' he said. They ran across to the rusty old estate. There was only a dog in it, barking at them, and the front doors were locked.

'No problem,' said the oldest Snarget. 'The back door don't lock. Move over, Shep!' he said to the dog as he opened the door and they all piled in. They sat in the steamy car that smelt of dogs and cows, and soon there

41

was a bang on the roof. A woman in trousers and wellies was standing outside with a lot of carrier bags. Her face was wet and cross. Norm opened the driver's door.

'Whatever are you lot doing back here?' demanded the woman. 'Didn't I put you on the coach?' She scowled at Lou and Barney. 'And who are them two?'

'The river over-flew, Auntie Flo,' said Arf.

'The coppers stopped us' said Ern.

'Barney and Lou got nowhere to go,' said Norm.

'Well, it never rains but it pours!' said Auntie Flo. 'Hallo Barney, hallo Lou! A good job I got some more food in. We'll go home the hill way.'

When they got to Starvecrow Farm it seemed high and dry enough, but the fields round it were drowned by sheets of water. They carried luggage and shopping across the yard, and into the big warm farmhouse kitchen.

A man with a red face kicked off his welly boots at the door. He spoke to Auntie Flo.

'The sheep and lambs are cut off by the water. If I can't get to them they'll all drown.' He glared at the children and went upstairs.

Lou whispered to Barney, 'Do you think they want us here?'

'Not much,' Barney murmured.

'Come on, fellers, let's go outside!' Norm said. The five of them went out into the farmyard. The heavy rain had stopped for a bit.

Ern pointed over the water. There was a little island left by the floods. From it there came the sad 'Baa! Baa!' of young lambs.

'The poor little things, I can see them!' Lou wailed. 'We've got to rescue them!'

'Haven't you got a boat?' Barney asked. The Snargets shook their heads.

'I wish — I wish Stig was here!' Barney said. His friend Stig would know what to do.

Barney looked over the grey water. The wind blew harder, a storm of rain swept towards them. Something black seemed to be moving in the storm.

'Look!' he said, and pointed. 'What's that?'

'A dead cow,' said Norm.

'No, it's swimming,' said Ern.

'It's a boat wiv some one in it!' said Arf, as it got nearer.

'It's not a boat, it's a bath,' Barney said.

'That ain't no paddle neither,' Arf said.

'More like a tennis racket,' said Norm.

'With its plastic cover on,' said Lou.

Then Barney knew who it was, that shaggy-haired figure dressed in rabbit-skins and black bin-liners.

It was Stig.

With a big grin on his face Stig paddled his little bath up to the farmyard. He jumped out and hugged Barney.

'Nice to see you, Stig,' said Barney. 'Ugh! — you're all wet! Look, Stig, we've got to rescue the sheep and lambs. Can you do it in your bath?'

Stig looked blank, not understanding. Everyone made noises like sheep and lambs and pointed over to the island and pointed to the bath.

Stig suddenly grinned, pulled a stone knife out of his belt and made horrible throat-cutting signs.

The Snargets laughed but Lou was shocked. 'No, no, Stig! Not hurt the poor little lambs!' And she made cuddling signs and crooning noises.

'Look,' said Norm. 'There ain't hardly no room for Stig in that there bath, let alone a sheep and all. We got to find something bigger.'

'Yes,' said Barney, and he stretched his arms. 'Big boat, Stig!'

They all gazed around the farmyard. Stig wandered off to the cart shed. In the corner were the remains of a light farm wagon. It had no wheels or axles, and, yes, it was sort of boat-shaped. Stig stood looking at it.

'That'll never float, Stig,' Norm said. 'It's all 'oles and cracks!'

But now Stig was looking at something else. It was a big new yellow plastic sheet, over some sort of farm machine. Stig dragged it off and pulled it out flat in the farmyard.

'What's he on about now?' Ern asked.

Stig was trying to drag the old bit of cart on to the plastic sheet, but it was too heavy even for him.

'I get it!' Barney shouted. 'Come on, everybody! Help!'

The six of them managed to drag the cart on to the middle of the sheet. There was enough sheet left over all round, so that they could wrap it over the front and back and sides of the cart and tie it down inside. Even little Ern saw the water couldn't get in now.

'Ooray!' the Snargets shouted. 'All aboard the yellow submarine!'

'Not a submarine, I hope,' said Lou. 'It's got to be Noah's Ark.'

Everybody jumped aboard, except Stig, who stood and looked at them.

'Ahem!' said Lou. 'Just add water?'

They all jumped out again, and pushed and dragged the boat down the farmyard towards the flood. Stig went off and came back with four long poles from a pile in the yard.

'What are them for?' Ern asked.

'You can't paddle a farm cart with a tennis racket,' Lou said.

45

Their Noah's Ark was afloat now and they were all aboard. They took it in turns to pole it, one person standing in each corner, steering a wobbly course across the drowned fields. They bumped against the island where the sheep were.

'Come on, sheep!' Lou called out. 'The Navy's here!'

But the sheep and lambs scuttled to the far side of the little island, and turned and glared at them.

Stig jumped ashore and, moving like a sheepdog, crept up on a couple of little lambs and grabbed them. He brought them back to the boat and handed them down to Lou, who cuddled them in her arms. Then he went back for more lambs, and dumped them in the boat in the same way. Even big tough Norm was cuddling three lambs. When the mother ewes saw their lambs on board they suddenly decided to join them and the air was full of heavy wet sheep leaping from the land into the boat.

'Well done, Stig!' Barney shouted. Stig jumped aboard and they pushed off. The boat was much lower in the water now, and heavier to punt.

They moved slowly back towards the farm. Standing in the farmyard at the water's edge they could see two figures, Auntie Flo and her husband the farmer.

Uncle Fred stared at the boat-load as if he couldn't believe his eyes. Barney felt he ought to do some explaining, so he jumped ashore first.

He said. 'You see, my friend Stig came here in his bath with a tennis racket but it wasn't big enough for all those sheep so we wrapped your cart in plastic and used that. I hope you don't mind.'

The farmer pushed his cap back and scratched his head.

'You did a good job, Mr Stig,' he said. 'So did you kids. Thanks!'

'How about pancakes for tea?' Auntie Flo asked.

Shooting star

Shooting star
Burning bright
In the middle
Of the night

Zooming through
The galaxy
On your way
To me, to me

I'll wish a wish
Before you die
And tumble down
The starry sky

That once again
One magic night
I might see you
Burning bright

Tony Bradman
Illustrated by
Gunvor Edwards

'Lonely Whale' (Green Themes)

One in a million

*Written and illustrated
by Michael Foreman*

Once there was a king who had all the treaures of the
world. His gardens were full of the finest flowers and
animals. At night he watched the stars, and would not
be content until he owned one.

A fleet of spaceships was built and dispatched. 'Be quick,' demanded the King, 'I want a star for Christmas!'

Just before Christmas they returned with a small star, but even this was too large for the palace.

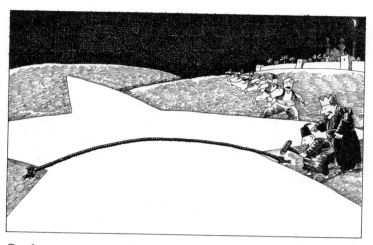

So the star was anchored outside the palace garden. The King sat all day and all night watching his star reflect the beauty of the sun and the moon.

In a distant city, a boy liked to watch the night sky. From his window he could see one star between skyscrapers.

Now it was gone. He became depressed and wouldn't leave his bed. Doctors were called and shook their heads.

The King's joy was beginning to fade. The star grew dim and looked as sad as a caged bird. Litter blew here and there across its face as vast crowds gathered.

Souvenir hunters chipped bits off, and real estate agents sold plots to hamburger and pizza stands. The cool evening breeze brought hurricanes of paper plates, gales of garbage, plastic blizzards.

'I don't want a rubbish dump for Christmas!' sighed the King, and freed the star.

It soared like a giant firework, to great cheers from the crowd. The cheers went to the King's head. He freed all his animals and knocked down the walls around his garden allowing the flowers to spread across the desert. He had the best Christmas ever, and didn't get a single present! And in a distant city, the boy could see a single star between the skyscrapers.

What is one?

One is the sun,
a rhino's horn;
a drop of dew,
a lizard's tongue.

One is the world,
a lonely whale;
an elephant's trunk,
a monkey's tail.

One is an acorn,
one is a moon;
one is a forest,
felled too soon.

Judith Nicholls

The Tiger Club

by Christopher Cox, aged 5
Westminster Children's Hospital School
1st prize

Christopher went to the Tiger Club with his Mummy
and Daddy in Wales. They stayed in a camper van and
it was really exciting. The Tiger Club is a nice place with
lots to do both inside and outside the clubhouse.
    Christopher loved it!
    Outside there was a climbing frame made of wood
with a big slide to slide on. Christopher used to play on
it everyday. Then one day Christopher came down the
slide and at the bottom he came face to face with a hairy
face!

What could it be? thought Christopher. He took a closer look and saw that it was a tiger. It was a very friendly smiley tiger. And the tiger said 'Hi Chris', and Chris said 'Hi tiger'. Then the tiger said 'Come on Chris, let's have an adventure. Climb on my back.' So Chris got on the tiger's back and they ran very fast to the clubhouse. They went up the stairs and opened the door, but it wasn't the clubhouse any more. It had changed!

It had turned into a beautiful jungle with so many different colours, red, blue, green, yellow and it was very hot.

Chris looked round and saw that there were lots of other animals. His friends were all riding on their backs, and the animals were all friendly too, and smiled and waved to Chris and the tiger. Then they all followed Chris and the tiger through the jungle, through the leaves, through the creepers and the twigs. Suddenly they came to a big dark tree, the biggest in the jungle, and as they went around the other side, Chris saw a magical sight.

Straight in front of him was a river, a beautiful, blue, sparkling, twinkling river. In the middle of the river he saw a crocodile. He was a bit afraid but then the crocodile waved and smiled and said:

'Hi Chris, come over here, I've got a secret to tell you.'

So Chris got off the tiger's back and walked over to the crocodile. The crocodile whispered in his ear and said:

'I've got a very special secret to tell you. If you look in the water you'll see the Tiger Club.'

So Chris looked and saw the Club far below. Then the Crocodile said he had a present for Chris, so Chris opened his hand and the Crocodile put a little Tiger into Chris's hand. Chris was very pleased with his present.

He was about to go when the Crocodile said:

'Chris, I'm wondering if you could help me, please?

I'm afraid that a lot of bad people are coming to the forest. They are going to chop all the trees down. When all the trees go, none of the animals will be able to live here. It won't be such a nice special place. We won't have a home any more. Can you help me Chris?'

Chris said, 'Of course I'll help you. I've got a plan.'

His idea was that they should build a wall. The biggest wall you can imagine, and very special because it would be invisible.

Crocodile smiled and said it was a wonderful idea but how would they build it?

'Easy' said Christopher. 'What you have to do is say ABRACADABRA, and put your hands in the shape of a wall.'

'Do we all have to say it together?' said the Crocodile.

'Oh yes,' said Chris, 'all the animals, all the children and you and me, all together.'

Christopher said, 'One, two, three,' and then all the animals and all the children said, 'ABRACADABRA' and put their hands like a wall. Suddenly the leaves moved and though you couldn't see anything, it felt like something big was building. All the animals and all the children watched, and after a minute Chris put his hand up, and he could feel the invisible wall. It was magic. Everyone cheered. Then Chris got on the back of the tiger and rode back. Chris was the champion, he had saved the jungle.

He got to the door of the tiger house, and the tiger said, 'I have to go now Chris,' and Chris said, 'Bye, see you again.' They waved to each other. He went through the door and he was in the tiger house. He felt a bit sad at leaving his friend, the tiger. Then he felt in his pocket and brought out the little tiger, and he had that to play with and remind him of his happy day in the jungle.

The sea

The sea is a gigantic man
With hair of wavy seaweed
His eyes are big grey stones
His ears are enormous snail shells
With one pearl for an earring
His fingers are corals

He wears boats for shoes
And a wreath of crabs and lobsters
He has a wet suit and trousers of sea fish
And starfish for his socks

He lives in a palace under the sea
Made of gold and icicles
And sleeps on a bed of foam
With soft sand for his pillow
And bubbles for his quilt

Where he dreams of sharks and monsters
Whales and an octopus and of looking after the boats
And what it's like in the upper world
Sometimes he dreams of punishing people and
Sometimes he thinks of saving them from drowning

He thinks he owns all the seaside
He has got no friends
He imagines a plug at the bottom of the ocean
But when he dies and dies and dies it will be poison
That kills him, poison and a great fire

Gerard Benson

Villanelle for the mermaid beneath Westminster Bridge

Beneath Westminster Bridge
the river mermaid draws a dubious breath.
She's had enough of this.

Her skin, once silk, is scabby now
so swimming isn't fun
beneath Westminster Bridge.

She coughs up diesel fumes
and lands peculiar looking fish.
She's had enough of this.

Don't wonder if you see her
slash the odd tyre before she slips back down
beneath Westminster Bridge

to thoughts of how she'll get her own back
for her lovely river gone to waste.
She's had enough of this.

'How about a flood?' she wonders.
'A party with my North Sea sisters as the cars
float off Westminster Bridge?
I've had enough of this.'

Whoooooooosh!

Julia Casterton

Animals

Animals live on this earth too
They live with me and they live with you
Please treat them as if they do
Animals matter

A big whale swims down in the sea
Down comes a net and catches it
We have got to stop before it's too late
Animals matter

We cut down the trees from the rain forest too
It's got to stop it just won't do
We destroy the homes of the animals too
Animals matter

Animals live in the woods and copses
We shoot them, the deer and foxes
Soon there will be none in those pretty copses
Animals matter

So help our animal friends
and maybe their happiness will come back

Jessie Holder,
aged 7½
Tiverton School
Hermitage Rd.
London N4
1st prize
Illustrated by
Maggie Glen

'Beyond the rails' (Animals great and small)

Elephant-lore

An elephant's brain is enormous
with a million things inside:
a portable memory, a space for sleep
and a list of foods to find.
There are maps and markers, places to go:
from Congo to Cameroon, to the
Ivory Coast,
an elephant's brain
goes like a train . . .

Don't complain if it sometimes forgets.

Katherine Gallagher

Eleanora

*Written and illustrated
by David McKee*

There was once a young elephant called Eleanora.
Eleanora had a long trunk. Of course all elephants have
long trunks but Eleanora's trunk was very long. Not very,
very long though, not long enough to reach the moon, nor
even long enough to go all the way round Grandpa
elephant, but it was longer than other elephants' trunks.

A long trunk can be an advantage. You reach just
that little bit higher without having to stand on a chair.

This is very useful because elephants are not very safe standing on chairs and the chairs aren't very safe either.

But long trunks can also get in the way. Eleanora's trunk was always getting in the way. When she was running, sometimes the trunk would trip her up and sometimes it would trip one of the other elephants. The elephants would shout 'Oh Eleanora!' and she'd say 'Sorry, I forgot'.

When the elephants played Hide and Seek, Eleanora would always be found easily because she'd leave her trunk showing. 'I can see you Eleanora' the seeker would laugh pointing at the trunk.

'Oh drat.' Eleanora would say, 'I forgot.'

When the elephants walked in line, nobody wanted to be the one in front of Eleanora.

The worst thing of all was shopping. Poor Eleanora was always knocking things down in shops and saying, 'Oh dear, sorry, I forgot.' Some shops even had notices saying 'No Eleanoras allowed inside.' Even now if an elephant is clumsy and is rushing about breaking things, he gets called 'An Eleanora in a china shop'.

One day Eleanora was lying down having a little rest and as usual her trunk was stretched out; along came Eleanora's Aunt Sophie and tripped over it. Aunt Sophie was cross and even shouted at Eleanora which is not a nice thing to happen to you when you are right in the middle of a dream about scoring the winning goal at basketball.

'Oh! Oh! Oh! I'm sorry, Aunty,' said Eleanora, 'I forgot.' Of course Eleanora really was sorry because having someone trip over your trunk is not exactly the loveliest treat in the world.

'I forgot, I forgot, that's all you ever say young lady,' said Aunty Sophie. 'Well we shall just have to make you remember.' Still talking to herself, she stomped off to see Eleanora's mother.

'I don't know what to do' said Eleanora's mother. 'I remind her as often as I can and still she forgets. I've never known an elephant forget anything before.'

'Let's go and speak to Grandpa' said Aunt Sophie. 'He always knows what to do.'

'Hmmm' said Grandpa Elephant after he'd heard the problem. Then he said 'Hmmm' again and 'Mmmm' and 'Aaaah' just to show that he was thinking because he was. When his thinking was over Grandpa said, 'It's most unusual because normally elephants never forget but I once knew another elephant who used to forget things. He tied a knot in his trunk to help him remember. I suggest that Eleanora ties a knot in her trunk.'

Eleanora was a very obedient young elephant so when her mother said 'Eleanora tie a knot in your trunk!' she did so at once.

'Now that knot will help you remember,' said mother.

'Yes, Mamma, thank you, Mamma,' said Eleanora and went off to play. A week passed without one problem with the trunk.

Another week passed and Eleanora was winning at Hide and Seek and running without tripping other elephants up and she was very happy.

After a month the shops allowed her back in and there was never any problem.

Grandpa was very proud of the success of his idea. 'You see' he said 'Elephants never forget, it's just that sometimes we have to help them remember.'

'Oh but I still forget all the time' said Eleanora.

'But how. . .But in that case. . .I mean. . . problems. . .you don't. . .if you see what I mean' said Grandpa.

'Oh the knot doesn't help me remember but it does make the trunk shorter so it doesn't get in the way' laughed Eleanora.

The baby elephant

The elephant baby was born in a zoo.
From his ears to his toes he was three feet two.
He sagged at the knees until his mummy
Curled her trunk up under his tummy.
His great big aunties cared for him
And his father taught him how to swim.
As he grew older they told him tales
Of a wonderful world beyond the rails.
His aunties talked of a huge wide plain
With plenty of sunshine and not much rain.
He heard how his cousins were free to roam
This fine sunny plain they called their home.
He stood by himself, with his little tail curled,
And wished he could travel that great big world.
He DID want to travel but what could he do?
He lived with his mummy who lived in a zoo.

Alison Jezard

A powerful wizard

A powerful wizard called Geoff
Was asked by a very small chef
'Oh please make me big!'
Then turned into a pig —
'Cos the wizard was ever so deaf.

David Wood

Riddle

I am
pear-drop,
space-hopper,
rest-on-a-tail;
fast as a rocket,
and what's in my pocket
small as a snail?
I'm shorter than elephant,
taller than man;
I hop-step-and-jump
as no creature can.
My jacket is fur,
my pocket is too;
a joey hides there . . .
I am

          KANGAROO!

Judith Nicholls
Illustrated by
Charles Fuge

Three Cheers for Charlie!

Written and illustrated by Pat Hutchins

Once there was a fat pink pig called Charlie, who lived on a little farm in the middle of the country. Charlie had a cousin, who was a fat pink pig called James, who lived in a little house in the middle of the town.

One day, Charlie said 'My cousin James is coming to stay,' and all the animals were very excited.

'I wonder if he looks like Our Charlie,' they asked each other.

Well, if they'd seen Charlie and James taking their baths, they would have thought they were as alike as two peas in a pod.

But when they saw them dressed, they soon spotted the difference.

'My word, Our Charlie,' they all said when they met James 'What a splendid fellow your cousin is. Just look at that hat!'

And they all admired the black, shiny top hat that perched nicely on the top of James' head.

And then they looked at the patched cloth cap that kept slipping over Charlie's eyes.

'And just look at those clothes, Our Charlie,' they said, admiring the long tailcoat and neat striped trousers that James was wearing, 'see how smart James is!'

And then they looked at the old knitted cardigan and baggy trousers that Charlie wore.

'And look, Our Charlie,' they said, when James tossed his silver-handled cane in the air and caught it. 'What a clever chap your cousin is.'

And then they looked as Charlie threw his wooden stick with string tied round the handle in the air and it crashed to the ground when he tried to catch it.

And when they had the barn dance on Saturday night, all the animals admired James. 'What a wonderful dancer your cousin is,' they said, as Charlie kept tripping over his feet.

And when they had a party for James, all the animals said 'Your cousin can do anything, Our Charlie, he dresses well, he dances well, and he plays the piano well. You're lucky having a cousin like that.'

And then they all said 'Three cheers for James! The pig who can do anything!'

And when it was time for James to go back to his little house in the middle of the town, Charlie said 'I wish I was like you. I wish I could look like you, and twirl my stick like you, and dance like you and play the piano like you. I can't do anything.'

'Come and stay with me,' said James 'and I'll teach you.'

So Charlie went to stay with James until he could dress like James, twirl a cane like James, dance like James, and play the piano like James.

And when he went back to the farm, all the animals said 'Where's Our Charlie? We miss him.'

'I'm Charlie' said Charlie. 'I'm wearing new clothes.'

And all the animals looked at the black shiny top hat and the long tailcoat and smart striped trousers with neat creases in them.

'But we liked your old clothes' they said.

'I can do tricks with my new silver-topped cane,' said Charlie, and he threw it in the air and caught it before it hit the ground.

'But we liked it when you dropped your wooden stick with the string handle,' they said.

'I can dance,' said Charlie.

'But we liked you when you tripped over your feet' they said.

'I can play the piano,' he said.

'We liked you when you couldn't' said the animals. 'We liked Our Charlie the way he was.'

'Good,' said Charlie, 'because these clothes are uncomfortable, and I like my wooden stick with the string round the handle, and dancing makes my feet hurt and I don't much like playing the piano.'

So Charlie changed into his old clothes, and picked up his wooden stick with string on the handle.

Then all the animals said, 'Three cheers for Our Charlie, hip hip Hooray . . .'

And Charlie did a little dance, and fell over.

'Hip hip hooray' they cheered 'hip hip hooray for Charlie.'

The ratcatcher

Written and illustrated by Errol Lloyd

Once upon a time there was a farmer whose farmhouse was over-run with rats. There were rats everywhere. In the loft, under the floorboards, in the cupboards, in the larder. They were even in the bedrooms. But what was even worse is that they were in the granary where he stored his grain and they were eating out his winter's supply of corn and barley.

'These rats will be my ruin,' he said. 'I must get rid of them at all costs.'

So he set rat traps baited with the finest cheese, he put down horrible poison, and he even got several cats, but nothing seemed to work. The rats always found a way to set off the trap then eat up the cheese, and somehow they seemed to learn very quickly how to identify the poison and avoid eating it, and even if the cats managed to catch any rats, they never caught enough to make any difference, for the rats continued to thrive and increase in numbers.

Eventually he became so desperate that he put an advertisement in the evening newspaper offering a reward to any ratcatcher who could get rid of the rats.

That same evening the ratcatcher, dressed in a suit and hat and carrying a briefcase, knocked on the farmer's door.

'I don't suppose you are the ratcatcher?' said the farmer, looking him over.

'I am the regional pest control operative,' said the ratcatcher who did not like to be called a ratcatcher.

'Yes, but do you catch rats?' inquired the farmer in a gruff voice, for he was never one for big words.

'I specialize in rodents,' said the ratcatcher 'and that includes rodents of the genus rattus.'

'Yes, but do you blinkin' catch rats?' shrieked the farmer who was beginning to lose all patience with the ratcatcher.

'I have been known to catch rats in large numbers,' said the ratcatcher, 'and I have come in answer to your ad in the newspaper.'

'Where is your equipment then?' asked the farmer who thought it a very odd ratcatcher indeed who didn't wear a white boiler suit and travel with a van full of equipment.

'I have just about everything I need here,' said the ratcatcher, patting the side of his briefcase.

Before the farmer could say anything, his wife who had been standing behind him intervened. 'Aren't you going to invite in the rat . . . er the, er, regional . . .'

'The regional pest control operative,' offered the ratcatcher who took off his hat and bowed to the lady. 'Thank you kindly madam,' he said 'most generous of you.' And with that he swept through the door and into the front room.

Before long he was settled in a seat in front of the

fire drinking a cup of warm tea which the farmer's wife had brewed up for him and eating cake that she had baked that very day.

While the ratcatcher drank his tea and ate his cake, the farmer had a good look at his briefcase. 'I don't know what you have in that briefcase,' he said, 'but whatever it is, I must warn you that there are hundreds of rats here, and you won't be paid a penny unless you kill every last one of them.'

'It is not my policy to kill rats or any other living creature,' replied the ratcatcher.

'I thought you came to get rid of the rats!' bellowed the farmer.

'That I intend to do,' said the ratcatcher 'but without killing a single rat.'

The farmer scratched his head.

'When do you intend to start?' he asked, as bad-temperedly as ever.

'We can discuss the details after dinner,' said the ratcatcher.

'After dinner!' shrieked the farmer. He was just about to explode when his wife again hurried to smooth things over.

'Of course you must have dinner with us,' she said to the ratcatcher. 'After all, you can't be expected to catch rats on an empty stomach now then, can you?'

'Indeed not, madam,' said the ratcatcher who reached for a second slice of cake. 'Indeed not!'

After a typical wholesome farm dinner of beef stew with carrots, dumplings and potatoes washed down by home-made beer and followed by apple-pie and custard, the ratcatcher retired to the comfort of the easy chair beside the fire (which unknown to him was the farmer's chair) where he had his coffee. After coffee he lit up his pipe and puffed away contentedly.

The peace and quiet of the rustic scene was broken only by the occasional sound of rats scurrying about in the ceiling above and under the floorboards beneath.

'When are you going to start, then?' inquired the farmer even more impatiently than before.

'I shall start on the dot of 5 am when I wake in the morning,' replied the ratcatcher whilst suppressing a yawn.

'In the morning!' bellowed the farmer.

'So you'll be sleeping overnight then?' inquired the farmer's wife for though she too was becoming somewhat impatient with the fellow, she knew the desperate plight they were in with the rats and didn't want to upset him.

'Just a simple bed will do,' said the ratcatcher. 'Nothing too fancy.' He then went on to explain that as the rats only came out of hiding after dark, he could only work during the hours of darkness.

'I suppose you can sleep in the guest room,' said the farmer's wife. 'It's the first door on the left upstairs.'

'Thank you kindly madam.'

'Mind you,' added the farmer's wife, 'there are probably lots of rats that go in there during the night.'

'That will suit me fine,' said the ratcatcher putting out his pipe and rising from the chair. 'I have an early start in the morning so I had best retire early.'

'Well, I hope you have a good night's sleep,' said the farmer's wife.

'There's just one more thing I require,' said the ratcatcher, 'and that's an empty bin' and he held his hands three feet from the floor to indicate how big it needed to be.

'We have just the thing' said the farmer's wife who went to the kitchen and returned with a large plastic bin.

'I hope this will do.' she said.

'Perfect,' said the ratcatcher. 'Absolutely perfect. By the time we have had breakfast tomorrow morning, there won't be a single rat in the house.'

'Breakfast!' exploded the farmer.

'My favourite meal of the day,' said the ratcatcher, who, bowing to the farmer and his wife, bid them goodnight and retired to the guest room carrying the plastic bin with him.

The farmer and his wife looked on somewhat mystified as he disappeared up the stairs.

Once in the bedroom he opened his briefcase and took out a pair of pyjamas, a ruler, a piece of cheese and a painting set. He placed the plastic bin near to the bedside table. He then rested one end of the ruler on the bedside table and carefully balanced the rest on the rim of the bin, so that the rest of the ruler overhung the bin, just like a diving board over a swimming pool. At the end of the ruler which overhung the bin, he carefully balanced a piece of cheese.

He then put on his pyjamas, turned off the light and went to sleep.

On the stroke of midnight, a rat squeezed through a hole in the corner and silently crept across the room in the direction of the bin where there was a strong smell of cheese. He climbed on to the top of the briefcase and from the briefcase clambered on to the top of the table where he saw the bit of cheese at the tip of the ruler. He carefully slid from the side of the table on to the ruler and started to edge towards the cheese. Once he got to the edge of the bin, the cheese was only a few inches away. He then set off on the last steps to the cheese, but before he could reach it, the weight of his body tipped the ruler forwards, and ruler, cheese and rat fell headlong into the bin.

The sides of the bin were too slippery for the rat to climb and the bin too deep for him to jump out either. The rat was trapped.

The ratcatcher woke promptly at five o'clock in the morning. He got out of bed and set to work immediately. He got out the painting set and clutching the rat between his thumb and index finger, he painted the tail of the rat a bright red; he then painted white zebra-like stripes along the sides of the rat; the legs he painted a deep purple, finally he painted the face of the

rat a fluorescent yellow before adding a series of pink
polka dots. As a finishing touch he painted the rat's nose
a bright red, just like a clown's.

He then took the rat over to the hole in the corner
of the room.

'Don't worry my friend,' he said to the rat 'the next
downpour of rain will wash this off and you will be back
to normal.'

He then released the rat and got back into bed.

The rat disappeared down the hole and dashed off
as fast as his purple legs could carry him back towards
the communal home he shared with the other rats. When
the other rats however saw this strange creature running
at full speed towards them with a red nose, a yellow face
with pink polka dots and with white stripes down the sides
and a red tail, there was panic and pandemonium. Rats
shrieked and fled in every direction. They ran out of the
attic; out from under the floor boards; out from behind
cupboards and from every nook and cranny where they
were hiding and the painted rat who couldn't see himself
had no idea why they were running away and ran all the
faster to catch up which made the other rats even more
terrified and they ran away all the faster.

They ran down the staircase, down the passage and in a mad rush they charged through the cat flap, through the granary where they frightened more rats and from there they fled into fields and all the time they were still being pursued by the multi-coloured rat who couldn't understand why they were all running away from him.

That morning over breakfast which consisted of porridge, bacon and eggs and sausages and thick slices of toast and marmalade and tea, the farmer and his wife thanked the ratcatcher. They were overjoyed at having got rid of the rats.

'You have saved us,' said the farmer.

'Have some more toast and marmalade,' said the farmer's wife. 'You must be ever so hungry after all that work.'

'Nothing to it,' said the ratcatcher modestly.

'You must let us now how much we have to pay you,' said the farmer. 'No price is too high after what you have done for us.'

'You needn't worry about money,' said the ratcatcher 'there is no charge.'

'But there must be something we can do for you.' said the farmer.

'My needs are few,' said the ratcatcher. 'As I go from house to house offering my services, I always get invited to tea and dinner and I get a bed for the night and breakfast in the mornings. The only worry I have is lunch. So there you have it sir. If you want to reward me, then reward me with lunch.'

'You'll have the best lunch you ever had in your life,' said the farmer.

'Thank you most kindly,' said the ratcatcher. 'Now you can, see why breakfast is my favourite meal. It's usually during breakfast that I get offered the best meal of my life.'

And that is how the ratcatcher came to have a sumptuous lunch with the farmer and his wife before moving on to a new job in the evening.

The sea otter

The sea otter lives where the icebergs swarm,
But his thick fur coat keeps him beautifully warm.
He dives in the water for crabs and fish,
For the otter thinks crabs are an excellent dish;
And it's terribly useful when you are able
To use your fur tummy instead of a table.

Alison Jezard

Ducks don't shop in Sainsburys

You can't get millet at Sainsburys
and they don't sell grass or weed
it's a total dead loss
for heather and moss
and they don't stock sunflower seed.

They've got some fish in the freezer
but they're low on rats and mice
and you're out of luck
if you're a debonair duck
and you want to buy something nice

'cos none of their bread is stale
and they've stopped selling hay and straw
Let's face it, if you were a duck in Sainsburys,
you'd be heading for the exit door!

Gary Boswell

84

The blackbird

There's a blackbird in my garden
Who has got the wrong idea;
It seems that no one's ever taught him how to sing.
He should sit up in the poplar tree
And fill the air with music.
Now that would be a really lovely thing.
But instead of that he perches
On the top of my old clothes post;
Well, there's really nothing very wrong with that.
But when he should sing sweetly
On a Summer afternoon,
He's screaming at the next-door neighbour's cat!

Alison Jezard

The snail

This is a song about the snail
Who lives on leaves and cannot fail
To leave behind a silver trail
Wherever he may roam.
He carries on his back a shell
Just large enough in which to dwell;
It may be small, but it suits him well,
It's humble, but it's home.

Colin West

Journey to the unknown

by Laura Soar, aged 12
City of London School for Girls
London EC2
1st prize

Picaval the Great! Picaval the Saviour! That was what they'd call him when he got back, when he saved them from the famine. After all, it shouldn't be too hard to find food . . . Suddenly, there loomed a huge cliff, right ahead of him, straight and regular, breaking off miles above his head . . . that was where they'd eaten before, inside that cliff. He hadn't noticed it ahead, standing there, grey and silent. It had no more food, so they had sent Picaval out, further than anyone had been before, to find another cliff. He gathered his courage, edged around the corner, and scurried away from it.

He travelled uneventfully for a couple of hours, until he reached the top of a mountain. At first, he could see nothing because of the blades of grass, about as thick as himself, but when he climbed to the top of one, he saw everything! Behind him, some distance away, he saw their cliff, no longer looming but tiny. Beyond it must be their home. On his right and left, he saw fields, huge insurpassable forests that now seemed undaunting. And ahead of him . . . ahead of him a huge place sprawled, close enough to look realistically gigantic, with cliffs tall enough to reach up to him on his perch, fat things, big things, and what looked like ants moved slowly between. It went on for miles and miles, even beyond the horizon. What a fantastic spectacle! A thundering, rumbling sound rose up from it. It frightened him.

Suddenly his light was blocked by a huge shadow looming over him. He glanced up to see an enormous bird hovering over him, beak open, malevolent red eyes staring — the next moment he was on the ground, running for his life, tumbling down the mountain. He didn't dare look back, but he could feel something above him. He ran, fell, picked himself up again, and ran. He didn't look where he was going, just shoved obstacles out of his way — until a huge block crashed down in front of him, almost crushing him, then slowly lifting again. He looked up, and saw a blurry monster towering above him, and looking round he saw there were more of them; and with them went a low-pitched rumbling sound, almost like speech, but so slow!

Picaval scurried through the moving blocks — he never knew where one would come down next and was almost crushed several times. He noticed the ground was hard, with no plants or grass . . . Suddenly there was a rush of cold wind, and a flash of black whizzed past him, closely followed by another. At the same instant, he felt an earthquake that shook him off his feet, then stopped as the black flashes passed. There was a smell everywhere, a terrible clogging smell, but in it — was that food? Yes! He distinctly smelt food, through the crowd of blocks, and beyond the path of flashes. So, he knew it was there, but he wouldn't stay an instant longer, in danger of his life . . . with a crash, another block came down, within a millimetre of killing him, and he ran again, back the way he had come, swerving to avoid blocks — and soon the blocks and flashes grew less and eventually stopped completely. And there ahead of him was his grassy mountain, if with dangers, at least with familiar dangers, and soon he would be home, home to tell the others of his world of blocks and flashes, and food! He should have brought a crumb home, for proof, but never mind. His family believed most things, and food was urgent.

Soon Picaval would be the Hero of the Ants!

The bug poem

Crunching and munching
Go bunches of bugs
      In shoes
      In loos
In milk in milk jugs
      In mouths
      Up noses
      On fingers
      Round toeses
On children in schools
On flies, around bulls
      In pies
      French fries,
On pigs in pigsties.
On some people's ties.
On plastic they're drastic
On cats they're fantastic —
(Gasp!)
Even bugs have bugs.

Hugh Scott

'Crunkle like a Florncake'
(Bits and bobs of nonsense)

As like as

As mad as a hatter,
  As bald as a coot,
As drunk as a lord
  And ugly to boot.

As brave as a lion,
　　As bold as brass,
As bright as a button
　　And top of the class.

As sharp as a razor,
　　As cold as ice,
As old as the hills
　　And not very nice.

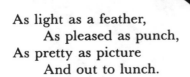

As light as a feather,
　　As pleased as punch,
As pretty as picture
　　And out to lunch.

Written and illustrated by
Alan Marks

Viola and the Ogre

by Joanne Brereton, aged 11
Hilversum
The Netherlands
1st prize
Illustrated by Raymond Briggs

I suppose you've read in fairy-tales how brave young men are always rescuing damsels from terrible danger. It's just one of those things and it seems to work out very well — unless of course there's a shortage of terrible danger! And that is what happens in this story:

Once upon a time there was a kingdom that was so peaceful and untroubled there was no need for damsels to be rescued from anything and it was dreadfully boring for them. Soon they began to grumble amongst themselves and the brave young men began to grumble too and eventually the grumbling arrived at the ears of the King. Now, he was a good man and he wanted everyone to be happy, so, he declared the second week in July 'SAVE A DAMSEL WEEK!'

'But my dear,' said the Queen gently, 'how can anyone save a damsel if there is nothing to save her from?'

The King sighed. She was right of course, but then she was always right!

'I have thought of that,' he said (and here he had a sudden idea) 'I shall advertise!' He then ordered the royal artist to design some eye-catching posters, which he then sent to all the neighbouring kingdoms inviting any dragons and/or ogres to come and settle in the area.

The result was very disappointing. The two dragons who turned up were so young and foolish that the King had to give them their return fare and send them home again. The only ogre to arrive was a sort of drop-out who didn't believe in violence and only wanted to be left alone, and anyway, he was a vegetarian. So the King gave him a nice cave and left him in peace.

Things really weren't going too well. 'Save a damsel week' arrived and still there was no danger. Tuesday came and went and so did Wednesday. It was truly a dreadful state of affairs. Now it just so happened that in the kingdom lived a certain young man named Thomas who loved a certain young girl named Viola, who loved him in return. This was very convenient except that Viola's father did not want them to get married because Thomas had sticking-out ears! Viola's father didn't care for the idea of having a brood of grandchildren with sticking-out ears. It was rather unreasonable of him, I agree, but we can't all be perfect. So the fact remained that Viola's father hoped that Viola would eventually meet and marry someone else. But Thomas was a nice likeable lad and he was sure he could win Viola's father's approval by rescuing Viola from terrible danger.

So, when 'Save a damsel week' arrived Thomas rushed about in search of some, but as I have already said, the danger just did not appear. If you are beginning to feel sorry for Thomas there is no need, because in between his sticking-out ears he had a good brain and he often used it. He decided to disguise himself as an ogre and carry Viola off into the forest, then nip home, take off his disguise, and hurry back to rescue her.

It was a clever plan and the first part of it worked perfectly. Thomas made himself a wild-looking wig by unravelling some rope. He bought himself a large joke nose and some sticking-out teeth and then made a tunic by cutting a hole in a large fur rug and pulling it on over his head. A club was easily made by knocking some nails into a piece of tree trunk and he finished the job by smearing himself with mud.

So, on Thursday night of 'Save a damsel week' Thomas crept into Viola's garden and hid behind some rose bushes. Next morning, when Viola came out of her cottage to go to the market Thomas leapt out of the bushes. Roaring fiercely, he grabbed Viola and dragged her along the village street towards the forest. Viola's screams roused the whole village and everyone crowded around in delighted horror.

Fortunately for Thomas no one raised a finger to help Viola, for all the other brave young men had got tired of waiting for someone to rescue and had gone fishing. In fact, Viola wasn't really frightened at all, because she had recognized Thomas's sticking-out ears and was thoroughly enjoying the whole thing. She carried right on screaming and Thomas carried right on roaring, although by now he was a little hoarse.

Just as it seemed as if Thomas' plan was going to work out fine, an unexpected snag arose, they suddenly met the real ogre!! He was on his way to market, carrying a string bag, to beg a few vegetables for his dinner. It is difficult to say who was the most shocked of the three. Viola and Thomas were very confused, but the poor non-violent, vegetarian, drop-out ogre was terrified!! He trembled so much that the string bag fell from his hand. However, for all his peaceful ways, he was no coward and seeing a damsel in such terrible danger he felt that he should try and rescue her.

The ogre jumped on Thomas and bowled him over. Poor Viola began to scream in earnest because she didn't want Thomas to be killed, but Thomas made no sound at all because all the breath had been knocked out of him by the ogre. They rolled backwards and forwards with a great many grunts and groans until at last Thomas's joke nose fell off. Well, the expression on the ogre's face when he saw that Thomas was not a real ogre, was so funny that Thomas burst out laughing and took off his wig and sticking-out teeth.

The real ogre now saw the funny side of it too and they both laughed until tears were streaming down their grimy faces. They laughed and laughed, slapping each other on the back so heartily that they both started hiccuping which made them laugh even more as they rolled helplessly about on the ground, glad to be alive and out of danger.

I'M AN OGRE!

Raymond Briggs

When they finally stopped laughing and remembered about Viola, she was nowhere to be seen. The reason for this being that during the commotion she had been rescued by a very nice looking, brave young man with flat ears. He had given up fishing having lost his bait. Now, this brave young man was, at that very moment, asking Viola's father for her hand in marriage, and getting it.

Well, Thomas cried for about a week and a half. The ogre, who thought quite rightly that all of this was partly his fault, tried his very best to cheer Thomas up. He told 'Bang crash' jokes (these are ogres' versions of 'Knock knock' jokes) and made Thomas vegetarian lasagne and nut-burgers to keep his strength up. Eventually, Thomas grew to enjoy the ogre's company — and even laughed at one or two of the 'Bang crash' jokes — and anyway, his cooking was better than Viola's!

So, the two of them became firm friends. Thomas would spend many a happy hour in the ogre's cave learning about vegetarian cookery and the ogre often came over to Thomas' house where they played chess well into the night.

It's funny really how well it all turned out in the end!!!!

A prince who went out for a jog

A prince who went out for a jog
Found a princess in tears on a log.
He cried, 'what's all this?'
And gave her a kiss,
And suddenly changed to a frog.

David Wood

Goldilocks goes home

Goldilocks, Goldilocks,
    Where have you been?
Oh, just for a walk
    Out on the green . . .

Goldilocks, Goldilocks,
    Have you been good?
Oh yes, Father dear,
    It was nice in the wood.

Goldilocks, Goldilocks,
    Did you see . . . bears?
Oh Mother, I didn't,
    Not anywhere . . .

Goldilocks, Goldilocks,
    Is all this true?
Oh yes, parents dear.
    Would *I* lie to you?

Tony Bradman

There was an old woman

There was an old woman lived in a shoe
spent her entire life
going round
saying

Poooooh!

Gary Boswell

Snippets

i

Jack and the beans talk
About the kind of thing
That you and I would not discuss
With a cabbage or a King.

ii

Old Mother Hubbard
Sat in the cupboard
Eating Jack's Christmas pie;
He opened the door
Gave a furious roar
And blacked Mother Hubbard's right eye.

Vernon Scannell

There once were two witches

There once were two witches called Win
And Min, her identical twin
Even friends they knew well
Were unable to tell
(fast)
Which witch was Win and which witch Win's twin
  Min!

David Wood

I woke up

I
woke
up
this
morning
feeling
really
thin

so
I
unzipped
my
belly
and
poured
some
padding
in.

Gary Boswell

The scarecrow

My name is Pat
And I'm very sick
At being stuck on a
Stick

George Abrahams
Westminster Children's
Hospital School

The big fall

I'm a leaf that came to grief, chief,
Fell off that good old tree,
Flittered and fluttered down to the ground —
Why did it have to meedle-e-dee
Why did it have to be me?

I was happy as a humbug in my good old tree
But now I'm all floppy and lost.
I get all soggy in the thumpering rain.
I crinkle like a cornflake in the frost.
Yes I crunkle like a florncake in the frost.

So carry me away to the compost heap
With a thousand other leaves like me.
I'll be happy as a hamster in the compost heap,
Dreaming of my good old treedle-e-dee
Dreaming of my good old tree.

Adrian Mitchell

Merry cowboys and a happy new steer

When I hear that magical cry:
'Scurf's Up!'
I rush from my hair-oil home
And over the scalp of the Dandruff
Sea
I ride on my scurfboard comb . . .

Adrian Mitchell

Keepers

Words can be very puzzling things —
Take 'keeper' if you've any doubt:
The zoo-keeper's job is to keep things in
The goal-keeper tries to keep them out.

Book-keepers are office clerks
Park-keepers lock iron gates
In Britain 'clerks' must rhyme with 'parks'
And not with 'Turks', as in the States.

The door-keeper keeps nipping out
To sink a quick one in the bar;
The lighthouse-keeper dreams about
Marrying a movie-star.

'To keep' can mean, of course, 'possess'
Though of the keepers so far seen
None owns, though all are more or less
In charge of ledger, bowling green,

Lighthouse, zoo or hotel-door.
I could continue writing these
Rhyming lines but any more
I'm sure would bring you to your knees,

Not in homage, but despair;
So I'll refrain from going deeper
Into 'keeper' words, I swear,
And you can be a hair-on keeper.

Vernon Scannell

100

'They turn into people'
(Other people)

Dad's dark glasses

sometimes when my Dad was watching the telly
he would fall asleep
and my Mum would shake him and say
go to bed Bob will you if you're knackered
and he would wake up and try to look alert
but one day he said the glare from the telly was
    hurting his eyes
and he would need some dark glasses
and from that day on
you couldn't tell if he was asleep
or watching the telly

John Hegley

Thinking

Susie was a silly girl
Her head was always in a whirl
Just crammed with bits of this and that —
Like was she thin — or was she fat?
Would it rain, or would it snow?
Or, did her slip hang down below?
Did her hair look best on top?
Or, should she walk, or should she hop?
And what to wear would drive her mad,
(And should she join the latest fad?)
Could she sing, or should she dance?
It seemed her thoughts were in a trance.
I wish you'd learn to *use* your head . . .
For more important things instead
Like — what do *other* people do,
Not only what is 'best for you'.
If you could look around and see
A bit beyond just you and me
You'd start to learn, and use your brain,
You wouldn't always just complain.

So — Susie tried and, do you know,
Her silly brain began to grow.
Instead of boring bits of stuff
Inside her head collecting fluff
She learnt to think, for her quite rare,
She thought of life — not of her hair.
She looked at other people's views,
She even learnt to read the news.

Her head's now filled with thoughts of sharing
Just *thinking* made her much more caring.

Nanette Newman

Tom's secret pea

by Joseph Browne, aged 8
St Nicholas at Wade School
Birchington, Kent
Illustrated by Posy Simmonds

One day a boy called Tom was in the car on the way to a restaurant. He was going with his mother, his father and, unluckily, his older sister. He hated her, she was always tormenting him, she always found some way to annoy him whatever he did or said. When they got there, Tom got out. It was the first time he had been to this restaurant. He followed his parents inside.

'A table for four please,' said Tom's Dad.

The waiter showed them to the back room. There was no-one in there.

'It's going to be a peaceful meal' said Tom's father.

'Yes, dear' said his mother. Tom sat down and looked at the menu.

'Great!' said Tom, 'they've got Yorkshire pudding and peas with roast potatoes, and roast beef.'

'Is that what you want then?' asked his Dad.

'Yes,' said Tom. 'Can you ask for carrots with it as well?'

'All right then. Roast beef with Yorkshire pudding, peas, carrots, and potatoes, it is, then,' said his father. 'That sounds quite nice, I think I'll have that as well.'

Tom's mother decided to have the special, which was chicken breast served with courgettes. Little Miss Tormentor, Tom's older sister, asked for the chicken breasts without the courgettes. The waiter came to take their order. They all ordered their own meals. Half an hour later the same waiter came with the food. First he brought Tom's mother's, then he brought his father's, then Little Miss Tormentor's, and last of all he brought Tom's.

'You were last, ha ha ha!' laughed Little Miss Tormentor. Tom looked at her and said, 'What's your name?'

'Katie,' answered his sister.

'What's this?' said Tom, pointing to his nose.

'Nose,' she replied, curiously.

'What have I got in my hands?'

'Nothing,' said Little Miss Tormentor, even more curiously.

'Katie knows nothing, Katie knows nothing,' said Tom bursting out with laughter.

'Stop arguing you two, we're in a restaurant,' said their mother, 'Now eat your dinner.'

Tom began to eat. He ate his dinner starting with what he disliked the most, and ending with his favourite thing. He was just lifting the last forkful of peas to his mouth, when he noticed a tiny little pea in the middle of his fork. It was so tiny it made Tom think, 'I would hate it if a huge giant were to come and eat all of my family, and all of my friends.' He felt sorry for it. 'I think

I'll leave this pea.' He thought about this for a minute, and then he ate all of the other peas, and got on with the roast beef. When they had all finished the waiter came and took their plates away, including the pea which Tom had left on his plate. 'Oh no,' thought Tom. Tom's father asked for the bill. When the waiter had gone Tom asked his father if he could go to the toilet. 'Are you desperate?' his father asked. 'Yes,' said Tom. He pretended to be desperate for the toilet. 'All right then, but hurry.'

Tom went in the direction of the toilet. Quickly he slipped into the kitchen and hid behind a bin. He peeped out and saw lots of plates all piled on top of each other. Great! He was in luck, his plate was on the top. Quickly, when no-one was looking, he darted up to the pile of plates and sneaked the pea off the top. Then he slipped out of the kitchen, back to Little Miss Tormentor and his parents. They were just paying the bill. Everything had turned out fine. He'd got the pea back, it was time to go home. He was pleased, it was his first secret.

When he got home, he ran upstairs into his bedroom. He had to find somewhere safe and hidden to keep the pea. Under his bed would do, so he quickly slipped the pea there, and went downstairs to watch afternoon television. While he was happily engaged in watching television, his dog Gilbert trotted upstairs looking for somewhere comfortable to have a nap. He went into Tom's bedroom to sleep on Tom's bed. He looked around the room, then he walked over to it. Suddenly he stopped. Something green had taken his eye underneath Tom's bed. It was very small and round. Now Tom's dog Gilbert would eat anything. He snuffled down trying to reach the pea, just one more move with his mouth and he would have it, he nudged a little and at last it was on his tongue. He was just about to swallow it when Tom rushed upstairs faster than the speed of

sound, grabbed Gilbert's jaws, forced them open and out dropped the pea.

'What's all that noise up there?' came Tom's mother's voice from downstairs.

'Nothing' said Tom.

Now that he'd got the pea back he had to find somewhere else to keep it, now that Gilbert knew his hiding place. He looked at the wardrobe at the side of the room. What was wrong with keeping it in his coat pocket? nobody ever touched that except himself. He opened the wardrobe door, rummaged around for his coat, put the pea in his coat pocket, and went downstairs again.

In the morning he looked for his pea, but he couldn't remember where he'd put it. He looked under his bed just to make sure that he'd changed the hiding place, but it wasn't there. He looked on the window sill, he even looked in the wardrobe where it actually was, but he couldn't find it. Then terrible thoughts came into his mind. What if Gilbert had got it? or his mother might have vacuumed it up off the floor. That would be awful, because the pea was like another member of the family to him. Eventually he gave up looking and walked sadly downstairs to have his breakfast.

'Is everything all right, love?' said his mum, 'you seem upset.'

'I'm fine,' Tom said. While he was eating his breakfast he suddenly burst into tears.

'What's the matter Tom?' said Tom's father.

'I'm fine' said Tom, trying to get the thought of losing his pea out of his head. After breakfast he went to school. He worried all day about it. At breaktimes he sat around on the school benches fretting at the thought of losing his pea. When he got home he was still worrying about it, his parents kept asking him what the matter was, and he always answered, 'Nothing.' He went to bed feeling unhappy.

In the morning, he was still worrying about it, and he kept on worrying about it for the next week and six days. By the following Monday he didn't think about it any more. On that Monday he went to school. At breaktime he put his hand in his coat pocket for some reason. When he took his hand out of his pocket again he was holding something very small, very brown, very round, and very wrinkled. It was the pea! He looked at it sadly. 'Oh well,' he said, 'I'll just have to get another one next time I go.'

Sunday

1
Ben fast forwards *Morning Worship*.
'Oh my Lord!' he moans
As Mum shouts down 'Your room's a tip!'
And then his best friend phones.

2
Simon tries to choose
Between History and *Spurs News*.
Tomorrow an essay's due
But this afternoon will do —
Spurs, then. The reason?
It's been a bad season
And we need your support, mate.
History can wait.

3
Dad is Mum's despair.
He slouches from room to room
With bits of the *Observer*.
It'll be Monday soon.

John Mole
Illustrated by Carol Thompson

Tim's tooth

by Heather Eyles
Illustrated by Wendy Smith

Tim had a wobbly tooth. It had been wobbling for weeks.
Every day when he felt it with his tongue it wobbled a
little bit more, until it seemed as if it was only hanging
on by the merest thread.

Tim was impatient to lose his tooth, but he didn't
dare pull it out himself. He had never lost a tooth before.

Tim knew he would get some money for his tooth.
'How much?' he asked his mum.

'Oh I don't know,' she would say, 'I expect that
depends on how rich the tooth fairy is feeling. How about
fifty pence?'

Tim thought that was quite a good deal, and he
would push the tooth even harder with his tongue, (it was
a bottom one, at the very front,) but it still didn't fall out.

'Pull it!' said his sister Sally, 'Just get a hold of it and
yank! I'll do it for you if you like!'

'Get off!' said Tim, 'It's my tooth and I'm waiting for it to fall out by itself.'

'Baby!' said his sister, but Tim noticed she wasn't too keen on pulling her own loose teeth out.

One day at playtime Tim was swinging as usual on the climbing frame, which was his favourite place to be, when — BOING! — a big boy's foot swung right into him and sloshed him straight in the face. It was an accident, of course, but it made Tim cry, and when he'd stopped crying and felt his face to see if it was all right, he realized his tooth was missing.

His precious tooth! His tooth worth fifty pence!

It was enough to make him start crying all over again, but when the playtime lady asked him what the matter was, he told her, and soon she had the whole playground crawling around on their hands and knees looking for Tim's tooth. His best friend Harry discovered it, under one of the benches at the side of the playground. It had flown out of his mouth and rolled all that way!

It was so tiny, just a little white pearl with a rough bit and a speck of blood at one end, not like a tooth at all. But Tim had it back and that was the important thing.

He felt the place where it had been very gingerly. It felt all soft and squidgy and tasted a little of blood. Tim didn't like that much, but he was so proud of his tooth it didn't matter and he knew there'd be a new tooth growing there soon.

The playtime lady, who was called Mrs Gibbons, found him a little piece of tissue paper to wrap his tooth up in.

'Now keep it safe,' she said, 'or the tooth fairy won't leave you any money!'

'I'm going to get fifty pence!' said Tim proudly.

'Well I never!' said Mrs Gibbons, 'that's just what my children get. But for their very first tooth they always got a pound.'

'Did they?' wondered Tim, 'A whole pound?'

'Only for the first one,' said Mrs Gibbons, 'Fifty pence after that.'

Tim thought about that all the way through his lessons. In fact, I don't think he did any lessons at all that day, he was thinking so much about the money he was going to get for his tooth. Every so often he would put his hand in his pocket and feel the little wad of tissue paper, just to make sure it was still there. Once or twice he unwrapped it in the classroom and laid the tooth on his table to admire it, but as it was so small it was so easy to lose and once it rolled right off the table and he thought he'd lost it again, until he found it under his teacher's chair. After that he didn't take it out of its packet again.

He didn't even show it to Aunty Barbara when she came to pick him up after school, for fear he would lose it again. He was saving it up to show his mum. And his dad of course, and his horrible sister. He'd tell her he'd pulled it out himself, not that someone had kicked it out for him!

When his mum came to pick him up from Aunty Barbara's he was so excited he could hardly speak.

'Mum, Mum, look!' he said, and he took it very carefully out of his pocket and slowly unravelled the tissue paper for her to see.

'Oh!' she said, 'how wonderful, Tim! I was wondering when that was going to come out. That's worth fifty pence tonight.'

Tim looked at his mum very hard. 'Mrs Gibbons says that the tooth fairy gives her children one pound for their very first tooth. A whole pound!'

Tim's mum frowned. 'A pound? That sounds a lot.'

'Only for the first one. After that they get fifty pence.'

'We'll see,' she said. 'Let's hope the tooth fairy's feeling rich tonight.'

You can imagine what Sally said when she heard Tim was hoping for a whole pound for his tooth.

'That's not fair! I only got fifty pence for my teeth! He can't have a pound!'

'Oh, for goodness sake, you two,' said Mum, who was extremely busy making sandwiches for a meeting they were having in their living-room that night. 'It's really not important!'

'It is!' cried Sally. 'It's not fair and that's important!'

'Oh Sally, I'll give you fifty pence if that makes you happier. All this fuss about a poor little tooth. You'll drive me mad, you children!'

Tim could see his mum was very busy buttering and slicing, so he decided to put himself to bed. He cleaned his remaining teeth, taking care to avoid the hole where his old tooth had been, and he got into his pyjamas. People were already knocking at the door for the meeting, so his mum and dad hardly noticed him go up. Right

at the very top of the stairs, outside his bedroom, Tim
unwrapped the little packet of tissue paper for the very
last time. There it was, the precious tooth. He bent his
head for a closer look, he breathed on it.

All of a sudden the tooth rolled right off the tissue
paper, right off his hand and began to roll down the stairs.
Tim couldn't move. He saw the tooth come to rest right
by a small hole in the floorboards where a mouse used
to live until a man from the council came and got rid of
them. Tim padded down the stairs after his tooth. He
put out his fingers very carefully like a pair of tweezers
to pick it up. Then,

'What are you doing?'

Tim jumped. It was Sally. Tim looked round at her
crossly. When he looked back the tooth had gone. He
had accidentally knocked it down the hole in the
floorboards!

'It's only an old mousehole,' said Sally. 'What are you staring at it for?'

'Nothing!' said Tim. He wasn't going to tell her he'd lost his tooth.

Nor could he tell his mum and dad. The door to the living room was firmly shut and they'd be deep in their meeting by now. Maybe it didn't matter. Maybe the tooth fairy would come anyway, tooth or no tooth. Tim certainly hoped so. But he wasn't going to tell Sally, oh no!

In the morning the first thing Tim did was feel under his pillow. He expected to feel something hard and round and shiny. There was nothing. He lifted the pillow. Still nothing. The tooth fairy hadn't been. Disappointed, he tiptoed into his mum and dad's room.

'Ummmmm,' said his mum, half asleep, 'What is it?'

'Mum,' said Tim, climbing in under the duvet, 'the tooth fairy didn't come.'

'What?' said his mum, suddenly waking up and sitting up very quickly. 'Oh dear! Oh dear Tim. I am sorry. She must have forgotten. I know, perhaps she'll come tonight instead.'

'She won't,' Tim said sadly, 'You see, I lost the tooth.'

'You lost it?'

'I dropped it down a hole in the floorboards. I can't reach it to get it back.'

'I see,' said his mum, settling back on to the pillows, 'well that explains why she didn't come. You have to have a tooth to show her. As proof.'

'Does that mean I shan't get my money?'

'Well,' said his mum 'I suppose I could give you the money instead, as I know you really did lose the tooth.'

Tim thought about it.

'It's not the same,' he said. 'It's not the same at all. I want the tooth fairy to give it to me.'

'I'll think about what to do,' said his mum.

Tim didn't have a very good day at school that day. Everybody kept asking him if he'd got money for his tooth, and he got fed up with explaining about the hole in the floorboards. Mrs Gibbons was the worst.

'After all that trouble we went to,' she said, 'and we spent ages looking for it. If I was your mummy I'd write the tooth fairy a note.'

'What kind of note?' asked Tim.

'Well, I'd write a note to the fairy, saying that Tim had lost a tooth and it was down a hole in the floorboards. Then you'd get your money after all.'

'Right!' said Tim.

He couldn't wait to tell his mum his idea. After tea he fetched a pen and some paper and put it in front of her.

'Write a letter,' he said, 'To the tooth fairy. Mrs Gibbons says it's just as good.'

'Does she?' said Mum. 'Mrs Gibbons seems to be full of bright ideas.'

'I don't think he should have any money at all,' said Sally, 'it's his fault if he lost it. And he's only to get fifty pence!'

'Now, let me see. . . .' said his mum. And this is what she wrote.

DEAR TOOTH FAIRY,
    THIS IS TO CERTIFY THAT TIM REALLY DID LOSE A TOOTH AND THAT IT ROLLED DOWN A HOLE IN THE FLOORBOARDS AND CAN'T BE RETRIEVED. IF YOU WANT TO VERIFY THIS, THE HOLE IS AT THE BOTTOM OF THE STAIRS, ON THE RIGHT HAND SIDE.
                    SIGNED
                        Mum

'Is that OK?'

'Great!' said Tim.

That night he went to bed with his note tucked under his pillow. His mum and dad didn't have a meeting that night, so they were able to read him a bedtime story and give him a kiss and things were all round much nicer. Even Sally was in a good mood as Dad had given her an extra fifty pence pocket money.

Tim couldn't wait till morning.

He woke up at daybreak, and remembering straight away he slipped his hand under his pillow. Nothing on that side.

He tried the other side. Nothing there either.

His heart sinking he lifted up the whole pillow.

Right in the middle, underneath, was a bright, shiny, new, pound coin, winking at him in the sunlight.

And beside it, guess what, there was his small, white, pearly tooth.

Children

Children
        as a rule
        explode out of school
They burst into rooms
And clatter down stairs
They run about shops
Do they stand at bus stops?
No they don't.
        They won't.
Can't
Shan't
Recalcitrant.
They'd far rather slouch
           or lean in a huddle
           or swing round the pole
           or splash in a puddle
They're noisy things children
              and messy
              with dirt
They won't change their socks
        or their socks
        or their shirt.
Then one day
They grow.
(Some fast
some slow
Some stay fairly low
some as tall as a steeple)
The amazing thing is —
They turn into people.

Hugh Scott

117

My relations

Somebody knitted my Aunt Julia,
started at the bobble on her blue wool hat,
needles clicking like ancient false teeth,
to the tips of her woolly toes.

She was popped through the door
of the cold, old house
where she lives today, without a budgie
or even a mouse for company.

Uncle Frisco was made by a Swiss toymaker
who took a month to put him together,
to paint his buttoned coat and shiny boots,
the parting in his hair.

He was wound up and set free in the street;
he came to rest at a bus stop
where he stood tut tut tutting
because the bus was late.

A Master Chef created Auntie Amber.
He decided for fun to shape a face
on an apple dumpling,
shiny currant eyes and a wide smile.

He baked her slowly in a warm oven
until she came out smelling delicious
with a powdery dust of flour on the pastry,
so nice he couldn't bear to eat her.

Irene Rawnsley

The crystal disc

by Claudia Zwirn, aged 10
St Hilda's School Bushey, Herts
1st prize
Illustrated by Bill Tidy

I once had a lovely, sparkling crystal disc. It was quite flat, but there was space to put something no taller than three millimetres inside. A piece of very thin paper would go in, but that was about it.

This crystal disc was magic. If I ever wanted anything, I just went to the glass disc, which was always in a tiny drawer at the back of my spacious bedroom. There was a minute space in the wallpapered wall. It was near the green carpet, so when I wanted the magic disc, I went to the back wall, slipped my hand under the pretty wallpaper into the small space behind, took out the wooden drawer, and removed the crystal disc.

When I was holding the disc, I had to put it between my first finger and thumb. My thumb had to be under the disc, my finger on top. It had to be my right hand. I then had to put my right arm behind my back, and turn around twice, saying the name of the item I wanted each time. Then, when I looked at the disc, that lovely thing I had wished for had appeared on top.

One spring day, I felt extremely hungry, but there was nothing in the kitchen cupboard that I felt like. I went back to my 1000 piece puzzle for three minutes, and then went to get a slice of hot, delicious chocolate cake from my magic disc. It was an amazing scene I found in my usually peaceful bedroom.

A slightly disagreeable girl called Carol lived down the road from me. She had heard about my crystal disc and come to see for herself. She had climbed in at my open window and somehow managed to find the glass disc. She took it out and looked at it. I learned later that she had seen me using it, and so knew what to do. Carol obviously wished for a gold chain with 'C' on, because that was what she had got. Carol smiled as she clasped on the beautiful piece of jewellery.

I could not stand it. Carol was using *my* magic disc so calmly and coolly without even asking me! No! Carol then got a diamond ring, and was just wishing for an emerald tiara when I sprang into my sizeable bedroom.

'Carol! How dare you? Hateful, horrible, sneaky, greedy girl! HOW DARE YOU?' Carol swung round in amazement. The lovely tiara crashed on to the green carpet. Then, Carol did the one thing she should not have done with the crystal disc. She placed her left thumb on the side of the disc.

The next thing I knew, there was a bang, a scream and a thud. Carol had gone! The glass disc had somehow, magically, flown back into its snug little drawer, and the jewellery had vanished.

What actually happened was that a small but heavy missile had flown out of the magic disc. It had hit Carol, who had fallen out of the open window. She had hurt her right leg, somehow got home, and it was a long time before Miss Carol came bothering me again!

The new boy

The new boy has many names
or no name he likes enough to keep.
He comes from Romania, or Austria
or Hungary, or Albania.
He's a cracker, he's funny, he's a creep.
He has pet bats in his roof-garden,
and a pickled dead scorpion,
and he hangs up the skeletons of fish.
He's carving a sarcophagus
out of ebony, and he says
he'll sail in it down the canal.
He likes air-balloons, too,
and he wears big-brimmed hats.
Sometimes we're not sure we hear
him right, as his accent's strong
but seeing as his Dad's an undertaker
we can't be completely wrong.

Matthew Sweeney

The Russian War

Great-great-great-uncle Francis Eggington
came back from the Russian War
(it was the kind of war you came back from,
if you were lucky: bad, but over.)
He didn't come to the front door —
the lice and filth were falling off him —
he slipped along the alley to the yard.
'Who's that out at the pump?' they said
— 'a tall tramp stripping his rags off!'
The soap was where it usually was.
He scrubbed and splashed and scrubbed,
and combed his beard over the hole in his throat.
'Give me some clothes' he said. 'I'm back.'
'God save us, Frank, it's you!' they said.
'What happened? Were you at Scutari?
And what's that hole inside your beard?'
'Tea first, he said. 'I'll tell you later.
And Willie's children will tell their grandchildren:
I'll be a thing called oral history.'

Fleur Adcock

A massive munch  (Food)

London fruitbarrow lady

The colours
fall from her hands

Yellows
reds   greens

She hides them
in brown paper

People buy

Katherine Gallagher
Illustrated by
Sarah Garland

Apple

Green round and shiny.
Freckly and smooth.
Good for a wobbly tooth.
It's nice!

Shady green like forest ground.
Shiny like a metal mould.
Round like a baseball.

It's very very small.
The texture of boiled sugar.
Juicy as a pear.
Sweet as my favourite fruit.
Tear it apart with your teeth.

Anthony Lowe
Westminster Children's Hospital School
2nd prize

I had . . .

I went to George's party today.
I had chocolate cake,
And fruit cake,
And sponge cake,
And carrot cake,
And ginger cake,
And cheese cake.
Then I had stomach ache.

Anthony Browne

Ill

I rather like being ill —
not *terribly* ill, but just a little bit ill,
lying in bed all warm and cosy,
after a tummy-ache or a chill!

The most pleasing thing about it
that I could mention
is that I'm the centre
of attention!

Gavin Ewart
Illustrated by Anthony Browne

Barmkins are best

by Joan Aiken
Illustrated by Susan Varley

Once there was a girl called Anna Freeway. She was not very big. Her father, Mr Freeway, was the owner of a huge chain of supermarkets. They were called Freeway Stores. Mr Freeway was very, very busy all week, running his stores. He worked in an office sixty storeys up. From its window you could see the sea, far away. But Mr Freeway never had time to look out of the window and see the sea.

Every Sunday, Mr Freeway took Anna for a walk. They always went Anna's favourite way — past the vet's surgery, where there were two big stone lions on each side of the door, past the war memorial where there was a big wreath of flowers, past the pond where there were swans and ducks, on to the common where there were gulls, and boys flying kites.

Mr Freeway never talked much. But Anna didn't mind. She liked looking about — at two pennies somebody had dropped on the path, at a sparrow that flew past carrying a bus ticket in its beak, at a man wheeling his rubber boots on a trolley. And she wondered about these things. Was the sparrow going to catch a bus, or had it just got off one? Who had dropped the pennies? Were the man's boots so tired that they had to be wheeled?

One day Mr Freeway was even quieter than usual. He was worried. By and by Anna noticed that he hadn't said anything for half an hour.

She said, 'Why are you so quiet, Pappy?'

He said, 'I'm worrying.'

'Why are you worrying?'

'Because I'm trying to think of a way to make people buy more food from my stores. And I can't.'

'Why should people buy more food?'

'So they can eat more.'

'Don't they eat enough as it is?' said Anna. She looked round. She could see quite a few fat people.

'Not all of them,' said Mr Freeway. He looked round, too, and saw quite a lot of thin people.

'What happens if they buy more food?'

'We get richer.'

'But aren't we quite rich already?'

'You could have a TV set in your bedroom,' said Mr Freeway.

Anna thought about that. She liked to sit watching TV in the main room, leaning against her mother, while Joe played tigers. Joe was her brother. He would have liked to come out with them. But Mr Freeway said that he was too much of a handful.

'I don't think I want a TV in my bedroom,' Anna said finally.

'Well we could have three cars.'

'Who would drive the third car?'

'It could be there in case something went wrong with the others.'

Anna thought about this for a long time. Then she began thinking about other things. How do squirrels *know*, when they jump from one branch to another, that the second branch won't break? What happened to knights wearing armour when they wanted to go to the bathroom? Suppose your arms started to argue with your legs, which would win? Suppose your legs said they wouldn't walk any more? Suppose your hands wouldn't pick things up unless you gave them a treat?

What *would* be a treat for your hands?

Anna and her father walked for a long way in silence. At last he said, 'What are you thinking about, Anna?'

She said, 'I'm thinking about barmkins.'

128

'And what are barmkins, may I ask?'

Anna thought hard for a long time. Then she said, 'Barmkins are things that I think about when I'm not thinking about anything else.'

'What do they look like?'

'There are lots of different kinds. They can look like almost anything.'

Anna looked round her — at the grassy common, the blue sky, the bare trees, the white houses in the distance, a helicopter up above, the red buses going along Park Side Road, at the running dogs, and the flying kites.

Her father said, 'Are barmkins good or bad?'

Anna thought about that for a long time too.

Then she said, 'It depends where they are. A stone is good on the path, but bad in your shoe. An ice cream is good in your hand, but bad down your back.' Looking at a tree upside down in a puddle, she said, 'A tree is good out of doors but bad when it grows up through your bath.' She thought some more and said, 'Joe is bad when he's awake, but good when he's asleep.'

Joe, Anna's younger brother, was clever, strong, and beautiful, but wild. While Anna and her father walked on the common, he was at home, hindering their mother from making lunch.

Anna's father said, 'So where would barmkins be bad?'

Anna thought, and said, 'Well they might be bad in a bowl of jelly, for instance.'

Mr Freeway said, 'Anna, I think you have given me a very good idea.'

They walked home in silence. Mr Freeway was thinking about barmkins.

Outside the vet's surgery, Anna stopped to give each stone lion a kiss.

Next day in his office, sixty floors up, Mr Freeway

Barmkins?

called all the heads of all his stores together. There were fifty of them, so it was lucky that it was a huge office.

Mr Freeway said, 'Ladies and gentlemen, I have thought of a very good way to tempt people to buy more Freeway Foods. We have already told the public that our foods are the freshest, purest, finest, tastiest, cheapest, and healthiest foods they can find anywhere in the world. Our bread is the best, our soups and sausages are the most savoury, our cakes the creamiest, our fruit the finest, our buns the biggest, our muffins the munchiest.'

'Yes,' everybody said.

'But, just the same, other supermarkets are now beginning to sell just as much food as we do. So now *we* have to sell *more*!'

'Yes,' they all said again.

'And I have thought of a way to do this. We shall tell our customers that all of our foods — the flour, the eggs, the milk, the fruits and vegetables, the sauces, pickles and relishes, the jams, marmalades, and spreads, the cakes and biscuits, and the coffee and tea and fizzy drinks, are *absolutely and entirely free from barmkins.*'

'What are barmkins?' somebody asked.

'Nobody knows! That's the great thing. But they might be very bad. Who can tell? They almost certainly *are* bad. And certainly they are not the kind of thing you want to find in your biscuits or your bottles of soda. Barmkins are bad for you. That is what we have to tell our customers. And there are no barmkins, no barmkins whatsoever, in any Freeway Foods.'

Mr Freeway's staff thought this a very good plan.

So huge posters were printed, and new labels for cans of soup and packets of flour, and for chocolate bars and frozen food boxes and juice bottles:

This Food Product contains Absolutely No Barmkins.

Then there were advertisements shown on television:

'Nobody wants barmkins in the corners of his refrigerator. You don't want barmkins in the larder, or the store cupboard. Barmkins may lurk unseen where you least expect them. Barmkins may breed at the rate of thousands every day. What can you do to keep barmkins at bay?

Unseen barmkins can damage your teeth — give you heartburn — upset the baby — spoil picnic fun. Don't give barmkins a chance! Always shop at Freeway Stores.'

For a long time, Mr Freeway's plan was a huge success.

More and more people bought food from his stores.

More and more people began to believe in Barmkins. They wrote articles about barmkins in newspapers and magazines, saying that barmkins were a health hazard, that they slowed down heartbeat and the rate of children's growth. Doctors said that barmkins might give you sore gums, or make your hair fall out. People began to say that they had *seen* barmkins.

Other stores soon began to copy Mr Freeway's idea.

They, too, said there were no barmkins in their frozen chickens or their instant soups.

Mr Freeway was very annoyed at this.

'I had the idea for barmkins first,' he said, forgetting that it had really been his daughter Anna's idea.

But there was nothing he could do about it.

For, quite soon, barmkins were everywhere — slogans on T-shirts and the sides of taxis and tube-trains said 'Watch out for barmkins!' Attention aux barmkins!'

'Achtung — barmkinnen!' 'Beware of barmkins!' 'Barmkins bite!'

By now, Mr Freeway was very rich indeed. He had four cars, seven telephones, and a TV set in every room. There was even a TV set in the bathroom, and little Joe caught a terrible cold, lying in the bath one evening until the water was icy, watching a programme called *Barmkin Blastoff*, all about barmkins in outer space.

Little Joe's cold started with shivering and snuffling. Then he began to cough. Then he refused to eat his tea or his supper or his breakfast. Then he was found to have a fever and a headache, and had to be put to bed. Then he became *VERY ILL INDEED*. Nobody but the doctor and Mrs Freeway might go into his room.

Mr Freeway and Anna were dreadfully miserable and sat about the house doing nothing.

'Oh why, why didn't I take him for walks?' said Mr Freeway.

'You said he was too much of a nuisance,' said Anna.

'When he is better I will buy him a TV set to hang over his bed.'

'He would rather come for walks with us,' said Anna. 'And talk to us.'

'What about?'

'Grown up things,' said Anna. 'Whatever *we* talk about. Barmkins.'

Just now, barmkins were dreadfully on little Joe's mind. He said he could see them in every corner, and that they were coming to get him. He woke screaming from terrible nightmares.

One night Anna heard him.

She jumped out of bed and tiptoed to Joe's room.
Mrs Freeway had gone down to the kitchen to warm up
some milk, leaving the door open. Little Joe was huddled
in one corner of his bed, with his hair standing straight
up on end.

'There's two barmkins over there, hiding in the
closet!' he told Anna.

She climbed on to the bed and held him tight.

'But, Joe,' she said, 'barmkins are *good*. Barmkins
love you!'

'Yes! To eat me all up!' said Joe, trembling.

'No — they don't! Barmkins are really, *really* nice!
They are gentle and friendly. They like to sing songs.
Shall I sing you a barmkin song, Joe?'

'Yes,' he said, rather doubtfully.

But Anna, holding him tighter still, sang:

> Beautiful barmkins, bright and busy
> Bubbly barmkins, frothy and fizzy,
> Cast your spell — make Joe well —
> *Now he's not sick any longer — is he?*

Just then, Mrs Freeway came into the room,
carrying a mug of hot milk.

'Oh, my gracious goodness, Anna,' she said, 'what
ever are you doing in here? You should be in your own
bed.'

Mr Freeway was behind his wife, looking pale and
worried.

'Joe was frightened of barmkins,' said Anna. 'But
he isn't any more now, are you Joe? Look —' and she
skipped across the room and opened the cupboard. 'See,
there's two barmkins in here, but they are *good* barmkins.
And they *love* you, Joe. In fact, they'd like to come and

sit on your bed and have you stroke them while you drink your milk.'

'All right,' said Joe, after thinking carefully about it. 'But tell them they must keep very quiet so as not to spill the milk.'

He drank the milk, and the barmkins kept quiet. Then he lay down and went to sleep. Mr and Mrs Freeway and Anna tiptoed away to their beds.

And, next morning, Joe was better.

'Pappa,' said Anna, 'you have got to tell everybody that barmkins are *good*.'

'But then,' he said sadly, 'nobody will want to buy Freeway Foods any more than any other kinds.'

'Does that matter?' said Anna. 'People are sure to buy *some* of yours. People buy an awful lot of food.'

'Well,' he said, 'I'll have to see.'

But already — somehow — the news had leaked out. Articles began to appear in medical magazines: BARMKINS ARE NECESSARY TO HEALTH. *It has been proved that a lack of barmkins in the diet may create severe problems.*

Barmkins are beautiful!

All the food stores began sticking labels on their cakes and candies, their chops and chickens and chutneys, their milk and margarine and melons, saying, 'Our products are full of healthy, natural barmkins! Nothing has been removed! No barmkins have been taken away. Taste the fresh real flavour. Barmkins are the best!'

And little Joe went for a walk on the common every Sunday with his father and big sister. He was a terrible nuisance: he chased dogs, and ran into the road, and picked up things he shouldn't, and wanted ice-cream all the time, and refused to come away from the slide, and hit other boys.

'But I expect he'll get older by and by,' Anna said.

And all the time they talked — about horses and helicopters and squirrels and submarines and Mount Everest and the moon and cheese and computers and sardines and Santa Claus.

And about barmkins.

Tubby tibbs

The strawberry cried
'I'm in a jam!
I don't know why
But here I am.'

The little tart
Said, 'So I see.
I know because
The jam's in me.'

And Tubby Tibbs,
The greedy lad,
Devouring both
Said, 'Just too bad!'

Vernon Scannell

The haunted sweet shop

by Hazel Townson
Illustrated by Nicholas Allan

Fiona Faddie would not eat
    The meals her parents gave her.
She always grumbled that they had
    A most peculiar flavour.

At supper, breakfast, lunch or tea,
    No matter what the food,
She always pushed her plate away
    In manner truly rude.

They tried her with:-
    Cheese dreams, custard creams,
    Sausage rolls, casseroles,
    Lettuce hearts, cherry tarts,
    Minced lamb, strawberry jam,
    Fillet steak, chocolate cake,
    Chicken wings, onions rings . . .
and the most delicious pizzas you ever tasted.

But all that wretched girl would eat
    Was what the sweet-shop sold her,
Until she grew so pale and thin
    They feared she'd grow no older.

Soon she was much too weak to rise,
    And there in bed she lay,
Dreaming of sweets she could not reach
    In sweet-shops far away.

'Now, this will surely cure the girl,'
    Her wise old granny said,
'For if she can't get hold of sweets
    She'll eat our food instead.'

Alas, though! Things were clearly not
    As simple as they seemed.
No morsel passed Fiona's lips;
    She simply lay and dreamed

Of:
    Rolos, Polos,
    Milk Trays, Milky Ways,
    Sherbet dips, chocolate chips,
    Matchsticks, Penny Licks,
    Munchy Mars, Yorkie bars,
    Pear drops, lollipops . . .
. . . and lots of other goodies, all in one huge,
  delirious dentist's nightmare.

The child grew thinner day by day
    Until her family feared
That in another week or so
    She might have disappeared.

The doctor called a specialist
    Who wrote a diet sheet
And said, 'If we're to save this child,
    Then here's what she must eat:-

    Sugar mice rolled in rice,
    Wine gums stewed with plums,
    Jelly beans on a bed of greens,
    Walnut whips in a ring of chips,
    An acid drop on a thick pork chop,
    A chocolate button on a slice of mutton,
    Turkish Delight on toast each night,
and a liquorice allsort sandwich every four hours.'

Their hope renewed, her parents tried
    With great determination
To make of this amazing fare
    A tempting presentation.

Flowers and best china decked a tray
    Spread with embroidered cloth,
But all it managed to arouse
    Was one more surge of wrath.

Weak as she was, Fiona seized
    Each morsel from the tray
And hurled it at her mum and dad
    While shrieking, 'GO AWAY!'

She did not even pick the sweets
    From their surrounding bases,
But flung the lot with angry cries
    Into her parents' faces.

'Right, then!' the doctor cried, 'A shock
    Might well be worth the trying.
'We'll set a scary tableau up,
    Connecting sweets with dying.

'We'll strike our desperate message home,
    Although it may be crude,
For a nasty fright is all that's left
    To change her attitude.'

They had a chocolate coffin made —
    (Dark outside, white within) —
Lined with a soft marshmallow bed
    Most gentle to the skin.

Its humbug handles shone as bright
        As any golden fixtures,
And on the lid Fiona's name
        Was spelt in dolly-mixtures.

There were also:-
        Poignant posies of Cadbury's Roses
        And bunched cachoux in violet hues;
        A fluffy cross of Fairy Floss
        Scattered with showers of Smartie flowers;
        And a 'marble' block of Blackpool rock
surmounted by a great big tombstone made of
    coconut ice with liquorice lettering.

This awful scene was set outside
        Fiona's door, and Pa
Said in the morning he would leave
        His daughter's door ajar.

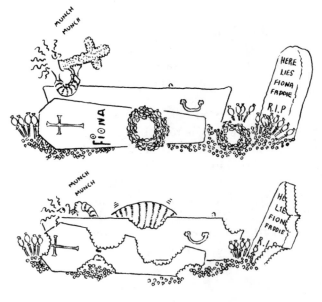

142

Yet suddenly, at dead of night
    Mouth-watering smells arose
Which drew Fiona from her bed,
    Following her tempted nose.

The scene upon the landing was
    A sombre one indeed,
Yet of its dark significance
    Fiona took no heed.

She recognized the tombstone's make
    And broke a corner off it.
One taste, and then the greedy girl
    Promptly began to scoff it.

She ate the floral tributes next;
    A very tasty bunch.
And then the coffin and its lid —
    A much more massive munch.

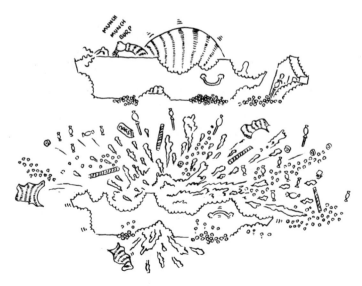

At last, when all was eaten up,
Her overworked inside
Exploded like a bombe surprise
And poor Fiona died.

Nicholas Allan
1992

And now her ghost is often heard
    In sweet-shops by the score,
Munching its way among the shelves
    In search of more and more . . .

. . . and more and more and more . . .
    Black Jacks, Cadbury's Snacks,
    Chocolate dates, After Eights,
    Spearmint strips, Ruby Lips,
    Kit-Kat breaks, Pomfret Cakes,
    Mints, dragees and Victory V's
    Aeros, Crunchie's, Bitz and Munchies . . .
And anything else you'd like to add to this list from
    your own delicious memories.

But when that ghost has eaten all
    The goodies out on view,
Beware! For if you're full of sweets
    It may well start on YOU!

An overweight witch

    An overweight witch called Priscilla
    Loved magicking sweet things to fill 'er
    Chanting 'al-a-kazeem!
    Make me an icecream!'
    She turned into a scoop of vanilla.

David Wood

Next please!

Please could I have an ice-cream?

Hazelnut, pistachio,
rum and raisin, strawberry dream?
Chocolate mint or chocolate chip,
toffee walnut, coffee cream?
Orange with vanilla,
raspberry ripple, blackberry flip?
Mango, lime or lemon,
coconut or cherry dip?
Apple, almond, chestnut,
apricot, banana cheese . . . ?

THANKS!
I think I'll have a lolly . . .
                    please!

Judith Nicholls
Illustrated by
Gus Clarke

146

The secret room

by Celeste Coates, aged 6,
Tyburn Infants School, London,
1st prize

The two little girls whose names were Sabrina and Serina went into a house where there was a library.

They read some books. On one of the shelves, one of the girls reached for a special book.

As she touched the wall behind the book, she knocked a button. And suddenly a secret door opened behind the books. Sabrina said to Serina: 'Let's go inside.'

They took some books with them to read. They saw a bed in the room. They had a sleep on it. When they woke up they saw a carpet was moving towards them. They sat on it and they told the carpet to fly them to America.

They went to New York on the carpet. They landed on top of a skyscraper. Then they went down in a lift. They saw a man who said:

'I'll buy your carpet. I like the patterns on it. Is it English?' The girls said no. So the man said he would buy them a hamburger.

The hamburger was magic. The man said: 'It will make you small.' So Sabrina and Serina ate the hamburger and they grew tiny. They looked like tiny babies. So they went back to the magic carpet. They did not like looking small so they asked the man to buy them a double hamburger to make them big again. So he did.

When they were bigger, the carpet flew them back to their room of books. One book was about New York.

'Oh look!' said Sabrina. 'We've been there.'

'That's our secret,' said Serina.

Please feed these animals

If you possess a teddy bear,
You treat it, I am sure, with care.
Each night you take it in your bed
And pat it on its furry head
And shake its paw and say 'Good night.
Sweet dreams', and then turn out the light.

You do? Well then, I have to say
That that is not the proper way
To treat a teddy bear, no, not
At all. There's something you've forgot.
In fact you've been extremely rude —
You haven't offered teddy food.

In future then make sure to take
To bed a decent slice of cake,
Some crisps, some biscuits and a jar
Of peanut butter, and a bar
Of chocolate for luck, and feed
Him all a bear could ever need.

Now if by chance your bear should feel
He doesn't really want a meal,
And doesn't fancy what you bring,
And will not sample anything,
You have to say 'Don't worry, Ted.
I'll eat it up for you instead.'

Dick King-Smith

'Fly to the moon' (Moving along)

The Journey

by Anna Mazzola, aged 12,
Croydon High School, Surrey,
2nd prize
Illustrated by Harry Venning

My day started bright and early at 6.00 am. It is amazing how early I can get up when I feel the need to. I was a little surprised at my parents' unenthusiastic reaction to my early awakenings, but, undeterred I headed downstairs to the kitchen where I treated myself to an extra nutritious breakfast; I needed plenty of energy for the day ahead of me. I ignored my sister's metaphoric comparison between myself and a pig, after all — my three bowls of cornflakes contained 60% of my recommended daily intake of Thiacin, Riboflavin, vitamins D and B as well as half the essential amount of calcium.

I dressed warmly, for the weather forecast predicted cold winds and showers. Honestly, it is meant to be summer! I again checked my rucksack and decided to add another two bars of iron-filled chocolate to my packed lunch.

I was then burdened with the task of persuading my parents to get out of bed. They responded to my efforts with criticisms such as: 'Dear God Heather, it's seven o'clock — have some compassion!' I had no sympathy for them whatsoever, if they chose to stay up till 2.00 am then they should be willing to accept the consequences of drinking half a bottle of sherry.

When I finally reached school at 8.35 I was highly miffed. When the rest of my family are in similar predicaments, I shall remind them of this incident.

I spent the next fifteen minutes discussing with Claire, Joan and Angela about who was sitting next to whom on the coach while most of the other juvenile members of my form went gallivanting off to the first and third forms to gloat about the fact that they would be running around the launch pad in the Science Museum while the other years would be slaving away in a classroom.

I was very disappointed with our teacher, Mrs Brocknen who arrived at 8.50 and expressed this to her. This was to be a commemorative day in the school's history — 'The Second Year's trip to the Science Museum.' She greeted this with a cold laugh. I believe that the new National Curriculum is ruining our teachers. I blame the government.

At 8.55 Mrs Brocknen announced a last minute loo call so that, inevitably, we ended up boarding the coach a quarter of an hour late.

Once on the coach John Roberts lectured the coach-driver on the dangers of smoking, the pupils were counted by the staff, and while a search party set off on the trail of Graham Gleenes, I read Angela's *Just 17*. Indeed, even before we had left the school gates, I had gained some educational knowledge. Apparently, girls of my age should have an energy intake of 2150 calories per day.

That sounded an awful lot so I ate a chocolate biscuit just in case.

By the time the coach left the school car park, we were three quarters of an hour behind schedule and Mr Langley was looking increasingly vexed, so was Laura Taylor who had forgotten her clip-board and had burst into tears.

As the coach approached the motorway, people at the back began a rousing rendition of Joseph and the Technicolour Dream Coat but were put to a stop by Mrs Brocknen for distracting the driver. Then she ticked off various girls blowing kisses to a group of punks standing by a bus stop.

At 10.30 Pete Oaker threw up into Graham's packed lunch bag on top of his jam sandwiches. The coach was stopped and evacuated while a rather flustered-looking Mr Langley cleaned it up and Zachary Ryder and friends popped round the back of the coach for a quick fag. John Roberts went to remind them of the risks of smoking. John Roberts nearly got his teeth kicked in. All this excitement was using up energy so I ate one of my sandwiches and then we were all ordered back into the coach before Zachary could ruin John's face (if you could ruin it any more) with his studded boots.

The next catastrophe was the air conditioning — not that it was our fault, but the stench of sick was making us all feel slightly ill and it was vital for us to get some fresh air before we all vomited over each other. Unfortunately certain people were not acquainted with such complicated technology and succeeded in breaking the whole system. Mr Langley now looked as though he was on the verge of a nervous breakdown.

We reached the Science Museum at 11.30 am only to be informed by tourists that it was closed due to a bomb threat. This appeared to be the last straw for Mr Langley who collapsed sobbing into the arms of Mrs Brocknen.

The coach driver directed us to a park where we could eat our lunches and we thankfully hurried there, hotly pursued by Mrs Brocknen.

At 12.15 the second year were rounded up and forced back into the coach. The coach driver then drove us back to the school on a fairly peaceful journey (apart from two people being sick, John Robertson being thumped in the nose and Laura Taylor sobbing because she had left her packed lunch in the park).

We returned to the school at 1.30 pm, with the exception of Graham Gleenes who seemed to have disappeared.

En route

On the way I heard Whistling Rufus
performed by a station porter
on a miles-from-anywhere platform
on the Norfolk-Suffolk border.

The wind and water of East Anglia
caged us in late winter; doors
slammed on it and we waited for
our time to come. Whistling Rufus

was six feet tall, raw-boned and
walked in a way that described porters:
he held his watch in one hand,
whistle in the other and as we

rolled away blew this chorus
between them. For half the length
of the platform his tune tied us to
bent grass and birds tumbling on

the teeming wind — until each note
broke away and we too were
blown up the same coastline.
I hadn't heard that tune whistled

since I was a boy: it was like
some great John Henry calling across
the flat sky to where trains turn
on timetables and old ladies doze.

Edwin Brock

On the ward

once when I worked in a hospital
one boy chewed the wheels
of another boy's wheelchair so badly
that it rolled along very lumpily
and had to be sent to the menders

John Hegley

Righto and Lefto

by Anne-Marie Watkinson, aged 10,
Ealing, London

In shoe land, where all the shoes came from, there was a message shoe. He used to be on someone's foot, carrying messages from place to place. When he became old, he went back to shoe land. He started an office saying where each shoe would go when it was born.

One sunny day in shoe town, twins were born. One was named Righto and the other named Lefto. They were black school shoes with laces up the front. A few days later after a long sleep the shoes went to the messenger, to see where they were going.

'Hello! let me see,' the messenger said, flicking through a drawer of files — 'Ahh! yes, two black school shoes. You have to go to Timmy Smith in England. Here's the address.'

Righto took the address.

'How do we get there?' said Lefto, unaware of the travel box. The messenger gave them a small box.

'Ohh!' Lefto said.'

The two shoes held each other, Righto typed in England, London. In a few seconds they were in London.

'That was amazing,' said Righto.

As it was early in the morning in England, no one was in the streets. So they got to the address with nobody seeing them. It was a small shoe shop with big red and white signs saying SALE.

The two shoes crept into the shop like a thief in the night.

'Let's go on this shelf here,' whispered Lefto. The shelf was in the middle of the room. They climbed on to the top of the shelf and fell asleep. A few hours later, at six o'clock, a lady walked in with a blue and white uniform. She was getting the shop ready for when the customers came, by fixing the till, tidying the shoes and sorting out some papers on a brown desk. By then people started coming in. Righto and Lefto were looking around the shop to see Timmy. Before they knew it they were put into a box and carried away.

After staying quite a while in the shoe box the lid was lifted. A small boy with brown hair and sparkling round eyes looked in, that was Timmy Smith.

The next morning the shoes were going to school on Timmy's feet. Lefto was talking to all the other shoes under the table, Righto got to kick a football. Three weeks after that Lefto went missing. Timmy couldn't find him anywhere, Righto found Lefto in a lost property area.

Since then the shoes went back to shoe land and made their own office of lost property.

Elegy

A thousand horns salute the parting day;
It is the rush-hour. In a solid queue
The drivers homeward inch their weary way,
And I am waiting for a 42.

Now in the distance looms a cheering sight:
As slow and cumbrous as a dinosaur,
A London bus is trundling through the night —
Alas! It is another 184.

But look! A convoy follows close behind.
Three buses, as if fearful for their lives,
Are travelling with others of their kind —
An awe-inspiring gang of 45s.

A 42 does not have many mates —
The species is becoming very rare.
Afraid to mix with 12s and 68s,
It hides in Camberwell within its lair.

A lonely, agoraphobic, threatened bus —
They really ought to put one in the zoo.
The Wildlife Fund should start to make a fuss
And issue badges, 'Save the 42'.

Perhaps it is too late. The one I missed
At five may well have been the last survivor.
An hour I've stood here, clutching in my fist
My 48p ready for the driver.

My rage has turned to sadness and despair;
A taxi costs a bomb, my feet are tired.
Tonight I shan't be going anywhere —
Hope and the 42 have both expired.

Wendy Cope

Genesis

My mother must have
pointed her out to me,
navy-blue serge
on an old black bike
on some grey winter day
when even the dogs were indoors,
saying: Look, there's Nurse
Winnie who delivered you!

There was rime frost on
the tarred road her black legs
flew over; her eyes streamed,
her nose glowed and she blew
white breath like a train
travelling between pains.

Of course I didn't see it
that way then: there was
just an old girl on an
old bike who waved.
The rest is written in by me
to make the event important.

And yet the nappy scar
which now sprouts a single hair
is true. It *was* cold,
and I do remember wondering
whether she was hurrying to
that great nursery where
all the gooseberry bushes grew.

Edwin Brock

Double bluff

by Helen Cresswell
Illustrated by Kate Aldous

'There is no point in your telling me Anthea has turned into a penguin,' his mother said. 'You've already tried that half a dozen times this morning, and I've told you — I don't believe it. Where is Anthea, anyway?'

'In the bathroom,' said Timothy. 'I've run some cold water into the bath. I thought it would make her feel more at home.'

'I see. Would you like some ice cubes? You could float those in the bath and make believe it was Greenland.'

'Good idea.'

He went to the fridge.

'Blow!' he said. 'Only orange flavour.'

He hesitated. Would these comfort Anthea if he were to drop them in the bath, or would she perhaps think he was trying to be funny?

'I'll leave it, I think,' he decided. He chipped off a couple of cubes and popped one into each cheek.

'For someone whose sister has just been translated into a penguin,' said his mother, 'you're taking it very coolly. Could you just move out of the kitchen? I'm trying to make a pie.'

'Is it a fish pie?'

'No, it's not. Why?'

'I was thinking of Anthea. They like fishes, all right, penguins. But I'm not sure about the pie bit.'

'This is chicken and ham. And I daresay she'll manage it when the time comes.'

'No.' He shook his head. 'She won't, you know. There's no pigs in the Antarctic, and no chickens. Definitely. We've done it in geography.'

'Perhaps,' suggested his mother, 'you might like to nip out for some whale meat?'

'I know you think I'm making it up,' he said. 'I told you — come and look for yourself.'

'And I told you — I don't mind playing games if I can get on with the lunch at the same time. If only it would stop raining and you could get outside.'

'Poor old Anthea,' said Timothy. 'I'll go back up, anyway. Somebody ought to cheer her up.'

'Doesn't she like being a penguin, then?'

'She hates it. She says the minute she gets turned back she's going to give me a real thumping. She's already had a go at me, with her flippers.'

'It was your fault then, was it?'

'We-ell . . .' He considered the question. 'It was yours, in a kind of a way. It was you who gave me that magic set for Christmas. And with all the instructions being in Chinese, how did *I* know what would happen?'

'I thought it would be fun for you to try it out for yourself,' she said. 'See what happened.'

'I did. And something did happen. Anthea turned into a penguin. I'm going back up.'

The penguin was standing in the bath flipping her feet disconsolately and sending up a spray that was landing on the floor, mostly.

'You do like it in there, then?' said Timothy.

'Like it?' shrilled the penguin. 'I hate it! I'm only in here so's I can get everything soaked and then you'll catch it. What did mother say?'

'She didn't believe me. Kept making jokes about it.'

'Jokes?' The penguin threshed furiously. 'Isn't she even coming up?'

'Wouldn't. She's making a ham and chicken pie. It smells ace.'

'What I'd like,' said the penguin — not exactly between clenched teeth, more between gritted beak — 'would be to turn you into a chicken and ham pie, and eat you!'

'Couldn't,' he told her. 'Not either. Penguins don't eat ham and chicken pies.'

'This one would,' said Anthea Cunningham, who had only an hour previously been a ten-year-old with long fair hair and blue eyes and was now a penguin, and might be for the rest of her life, for all she knew.

'I'm sorry,' said Timothy. 'I really am beginning to feel sorry for you.'

'Thank you very much,' said the penguin, with a swift swipe of a flipper that caught him wetly behind the ear. He ducked back.

'If you're going to be like that,' he said, 'I shan't even try to help. And it was as much your fault as mine — you can't read Chinese any more than I can. And you're older than me. If you'd been able to read Chinese this would never have happened.'

'You'll be saying next,' said the penguin, 'that if I hadn't been born in the first place this would never have happened!'

Timothy thought for a moment.

'Well, it wouldn't, would it? Come to think of it.'

160

His words were greeted with the wettest yet spray of cold water.

'The only thing I can think of,' he said, 'is to try something else out of the box. See what happens. If there's a spell for turning people into penguins, there ought to be one for turning them back again. Else people would want their money back.'

'That's true,' she agreed. 'That's the first sensible remark you've made today.'

'I'll get it.'

Timothy laid the large box as far as possible from the spray area. He did not want water in his spells.

'The trouble is . . . what? I mean, it could be any of these.'

'Try the one next to it,' suggested Anthea.

'It's a bit of a bright colour,' said Timothy dubiously.

'All the more likely to work. Go on. Do it. Sprinkle some over me, like you did with the other stuff.'

'But what if it turned you *into* that colour?'

'Oh don't be stupid!' snapped the penguin. 'Whoever heard of a pink penguin? Go on, do it!'

'Promise not to splash while I'm doing it?'

'Promise.'

Timothy advanced towards the bath, then unstoppered the phial of pink powder and held it poised. Just before sprinkling it, he did what he had been longing to do all morning — he actually touched the penguin's silky head.

'Gosh!' he thought. 'It *is* a penguin — actually!'

He sprinkled a little shower of the pink dust over the dark head, shut his eyes, tapped three times with the little ivory wand and said a spell three times very quickly. Then he took a step backwards and opened his eyes. He yelped and leapt back again.

The penguin was a bright flamingo pink. Only its little gold eyes remained unchanged.

'Oh, *now* we've done it!'

It seemed to Timothy that while his parents might have become reconciled in time to the idea of a penguin in the family, they were going to draw the line at this foreign-looking, rather stout bird in shocking pink.

'You — wait!' The words came out as a hiss and he backed away again and trod on the magic box.

'I'm sorry — I really am! You look *awful* now — horrible! But it was you that made me do it.'

The penguin began to cry.

'You've ruined my whole l-life!' it sobbed. 'Now what will happen to me? At least before I could have gone and lived in a zoo, and had an ordinary sort of life! But now I'm a f-f-freak!'

'You certainly are,' agreed Timothy fervently. 'I honestly have never seen such a horrible sight in my life.'

'Ooooh!' The pink penguin's wail went high and desperate.

'I think Mother *had* better come up.'

He went back downstairs. He sniffed appreciatively as he entered the kitchen.

'*That* smells good!' and he felt sorrier than ever for his pink sister.

'How's the penguin?' asked his mother.

'That's what I've come about. It's got worse than ever now. She's gone a horrible bright pink — you know, sort of fluorescent, like you see on posters.'

'Pink *and* a penguin?' she enquired. 'Or just pink?'

'Both. She's crying now, and I don't blame her. I think you ought to go up and comfort her.'

'If I go upstairs and find a bright pink penguin in my bathroom,' she said, 'I'm more likely to faint than start comforting.'

'It's certainly enough to make anyone faint. But in a way, she's lucky. I mean, for instance, she'll never have to go to school again. Or practise the piano. I think once she gets used to the idea, she'll see the advantages.'

'Would you just go up and tell her,' said his mother, 'that I'm dishing up in five minutes?'

'Gosh!' came a voice behind them. 'That smells gorgeous!'

Timothy turned. Anthea smiled at him.

'You — you've turned back!' he said accusingly.

'I've — what?'

'Changed back.'

'What from?'

'From a pink penguin, of course!'

'Pink penguin? What *are* you talking about?'

'It's a game he's been having, dear,' said their mother. 'I've been getting bulletins on you all morning. Last time

I heard you were a phosphorescent pink penguin in floods of tears.'

'Honestly!' Anthea put on her superior face. 'You do think of the most ridiculous games!'

'If you can't remember,' said Timothy stubbornly, 'then all I can say is, that the spell must have made you lose your memory, as well. Yes, I expect that's it. You wait till you get your next test at school. You won't be able to remember a thing.'

'Idiot!' She turned away.

Timothy turned to his mother.

'Look,' he said, 'who do you believe? Her or me?'

She hesitated.

'We'll put it this way,' she said. 'As soon as we've had lunch and washed up, if it's still raining and you can't go out, I'll let you try a spell on me. How would that do?'

A slow smile spread over his face.

'Oh, that will be very good,' he said. 'Very good indeed.'

And with that he went into a corner and began to sing, under his breath, an African rain chant that had never let him down yet . . .

My first friends

by Nicola Complin, aged 13, Croydon High, Selsdon,
3rd prize

Tuesday

Dear Diary, today was the day I went to my new school. The school ship came at the rise of the fourth moon, it was bigger than I had expected and the journey was longer.

I am going to be aboard the ship for 4 days. I was the first one to be picked up. We were going to stop at Azlainia next. I've never been to another planet or school and my only friend was Jessy my robot, as my parents had always preferred me to have a private tutor, so I have never met anyone my own age.

The only people I have met aboard the ship are the robots so I'm still really excited about meeting my first friend and I can't help wondering what he or she is going to be like.

Wednesday

I met my room-mate today. Her name is Nebular. It was a bit of a shock when I first saw her as she does not look like anyone I've ever seen before. She is leonine, but has a pure beauty that shines through. I have drawn a picture of her, but I am afraid it is not very good and does not do her justice.

Nebular does not speak English but I still seem to be able to understand her. I'm not sure how to explain but I will try . . . It's like she pushes what she is saying into my brain and forces my mind to translate.

At lunch time the robot told us that our next stop would be K'Kreez. When she said this Nebular's face darkened. I asked her why, and she began telling me about the History of Aslan.

'My race were innocent, for we only used to hunt for food, then the K'Kree race came and killed many of

165

my own people because they wanted our sacred sand which is not really sand but many jewels so the K'Kree are hated by Aslainians.'

'Oh but wasn't that a long time ago?' I asked, shocked by what she said.

'Yes but people don't change, and besides I was taught to hate them. It's like a tradition.'

'What do they look like,' I asked quietly.

'Like what you used to call dinosaurs. They are about 6 foot when they are fully grown.' This ended our conversation as I saw that she did not want to carry on.

Thursday

I didn't believe Nebular when she said the K'Kree were like dinosaurs but they are! The K'Kree on board is called Hiver, he is the son of the crowned prince and he speaks 74 languages which includes space English and Azlainian.

To start with, when Nebby and Hiver were in the same room, you could cut the atmosphere with a knife, but, as the day wore on, Hiver and Nebby began talking and Nebby agreed that you can't judge someone by their ancestors.

Friday

It was our last day on board today and we were going to meet our last best friend. He is a droyne.

He is quiet but caring. He has a power of healing. We found this out when I cut myself and started crying without a word. Magyor (that was the Droynes' name) came over and touched my hand, then my cut and, as I watched, it healed. He looked up with a gleam in his eye as if he was pleased that I was not crying any more. As I went to say thank you he teleported back to his seat, all without saying a word.

Tonight, I don't know if I want to go back to sleep because when I wake up I am afraid that I will be back home with only my robot for a friend.

There once was a witch

There once was witch called June
Who started to fly to the moon
But after an hour
Her broomstick lost power
And she got back to earth — rather soon!

David Wood
Illustrated by Doffy Weir

Doffy Weir

My Magic Carpet Secret

*By Jennifer Fahey, aged 5,
Tyburn Infants school, London,
2nd prize.
Illustrated by Benedict Blathwayt*

I went on the magic carpet and I saw the clouds in the sky.

The carpet landed on the cloud. Joanne got on the carpet and all the birds were singing.

The birds said, 'Tweet, tweet,' and asked her to come and sing with them.

But Joanne said, 'Come with me on my magic carpet, if you can keep a secret.'

All the birds said, 'Yes please.' So they jumped on the magic carpet with Joanne. The carpet took them to Regents Park and landed in the Monkey House. The monkeys said, 'Hello.'

The monkeys said, 'Can we come too?'

So one by one the monkeys sat on the mat with her. The monkeys said, 'Can we fly over a rainbow?'

So the carpet took them over a beautiful rainbow.

The magic carpet was our secret. It took us wherever we wanted to go, and wherever our friends the birds and the monkeys wanted to go.

They never told anyone about our secret and neither did we. Not for ever and ever.

'Throw your head like a beachball' (It's magic)

Jasper the vain toucan

by Angela McAllister
Illustrated by Susie Jenkin-Pearce

Jasper was a vain toucan who plumed and preened and peered at his reflection all day long.

He was especially proud of his beautiful beak which he polished with great care and displayed for all the creatures of the jungle to admire as he swaggered splendidly by.

All the creatures of the jungle thought Jasper was quite silly.

'A beak is for catching food', they said disapprovingly.

But Jasper was so proud of his beak that he wouldn't use it to catch food in case it got scratched and dirty.

So the other toucans shared their food with Jasper.

'He may be quite silly, but we birds of a feather must stick together,' they agreed. 'One day Jasper will change. . . .'

But Jasper only changed for the worse!

He became more and more boastful of his handsome beak. Every day he posed grandly on a rock in the middle of the river to be more easily admired from all sides.

One afternoon as he gazed at his reflection in the water Jasper had an outrageous idea. 'If I had a beak of GOLD I would dazzle everybody with my brilliance!' he thought excitedly. 'Then nobody could deny I was the most magnificent bird in the whole jungle!'

But where was he to find a beak of gold?

Jasper remembered something he had heard about a Miracle Bird who lived deep in the heart of the jungle.

The Miracle Bird was as old as the ancient rivers and could do strange and wonderful things.

'Maybe he could give me a beak of gold' thought Jasper.

So he set off into the heart of the jungle to find the Miracle Bird.

As he searched the deep darkness Jasper came to a clearing lit by a single shaft of light. And there on a knot of tangled roots sat the Miracle Bird.

Jasper had expected to find a fabulous creature with bright feathers and a magnificent tail. But instead he was surprised to see a small black bird with one curled tail feather and sleepy green eyes. Jasper introduced himself and explained that he was looking for a gold beak.

The Miracle Bird blinked dreamily.

'Are you *sure* you want a gold beak?' he asked.

'Oh yes, more than anything, I do want a gold beak' answered Jasper eagerly.

'More than *anything*?' said the Miracle Bird, peering at the toucan closely.

Jasper could not think of anything better than being the most handsome creature in the jungle. 'More than ANYTHING!' he insisted.

'Well, I think you are being quite silly. . .' said the Miracle Bird, 'but if that is what you really want you must eat the fruit of this ancient Orinoco tree and drink the water where the sunlight falls.'

Jasper was too excited about his beak to consider whether he was being quite silly. He ate the fruit and drank from the sunlit water and waited impatiently for something to happen.

'Don't just stand there like a toucan. . .' said the Miracle Bird wearily.

'But I am a toucan!' replied Jasper, staring hard at his beak.

'. . . You may return home. And by the time you arrive you will have a beak of pure gold,' promised the Miracle Bird, and with a deep sigh he shut his eyes and went to sleep.

Jasper set off home, full of expectation. And, as he flew among the giant trees of the jungle, his beak caught the light and shone brighter and brighter.

But as it grew golden it also grew heavy, and soon Jasper was too heavy to fly.

So he continued his journey on foot. But the beautiful gold beak weighed heavier and heavier until he could hardly lift his head from the ground. Finally, as he came to a slimey swamp, Jasper's gold beak glinted brilliantly and then sank deep into the mud. And no matter how hard he tugged he could not pull himself free. Jasper felt quite silly standing on tiptoes with his beak in the mud,

Snaig Jenkin-Pearce.

looking at the world upside down. 'I do hope nobody comes along and sees me like this' he thought.

But as the day passed, Jasper started to feel bored and lonely. He tried tugging again but the gold beak was firmly stuck in the mud and too heavy to pull out.

Jasper wished he was back on the rock in the middle of the river with his old polished beak in all its glory . . .

The day passed and the night came and poor Jasper had to sleep on his tiptoes, upside down.

In the morning he was hungry but there was nobody

to pull him out and feed him. Soon he started to look thin and ragged and muddy.

'I wish I didn't have this heavy gold beak,' sighed Jasper to himself, 'I wish I had my old beak back. More than anything I wish I had an ordinary toucan's beak . . .'

'More than *anything*?' said a small voice from the undergrowth.

Poor Jasper couldn't look up but he heard a rustle of leaves and there before him he saw the tiny black feet of the Miracle Bird.

Jasper couldn't think of anything better than being an ordinary toucan with a beak light enough for flying and perfect for catching food — no matter *what* it looked like.

'More than ANYTHING!' he said in his muffled voice.

'Well, let that be an end to all this nonsense' said the Miracle Bird kindly.

And with a jerk Jasper fell back out of the swamp, pulling his old beak out of the mud.

'I have been quite silly, haven't I?' said Jasper shyly as he accustomed himself to being downside up again.

'You *were* quite silly but now you have changed' the Miracle Bird assured him. And with a wink of his bright eye he hopped off back to the heart of the jungle.

At last Jasper flew home light and free. When the other toucans saw him they hardly recognized the thin, ragged, muddy bird before them.

But Jasper would not tell anyone about his quite silly adventure. 'I shan't be going on any more journeys' he told them. 'I've had enough change for one toucan. And after all, we ordinary birds of a feather must stick together.'

And he flew off to gather food for them all to share . . .

The wizard that was

his pointed hat is pointless
his magic wand's a stick
his dog could do better tricks with
if she hadn't run away
he can say every word the spell book says to say
and wave his arms about all day
but he's powerless
he couldn't cast a shepherd
in a school nativity play

John Hegley

The two wizards

by Louisa Wood, aged 8,
Combe Bank Preparatory School,
2nd prize.

Once there lived a wizard called Hoggle. Hoggle was a
very fat wizard and he had warts all over him and on his
eyelids little toadstools were growing. He lived in a cave
with a rat, a snake, a pig and a lizard. At the back of
his cave was a cupboard with all the stuff for making spells
like: eyeball
    blood
    juice
    slime
    and lots more. In the middle was a bed and a
cauldron. His bed was full of fleas, mice, rats and snails.
How Hoggle slept, I do not know.

Now Hoggle had a friend called Hairy. Hairy was also fat and short but instead of warts he had hair and he did not live with a rat, a snake, a pig and a lizard. He lived with a pig, a lizard, a rat and a snake. Hairy and Hoggle thought that if an animal was in a different order they were different animals.

Now Hairy and Hoggle liked playing tricks on each other and one day Hoggle decided to turn Hairy into a porcupine.

'What fun it will be,' he said.

So he began to make a potion. Little did he know that Hairy was saying the same thing, 'We'll turn him into a toad. What fun it will be.' Hoggle went to Hairy's house to have tea and when Hairy was out he put the potion into Hairy's food and the rest in his water. And when Hoggle was not looking Hairy put the potion in his food. When they sat down for tea the wizards thought, 'this is it'.

!!!Zittttletttlepom!!! went the potion. There was a porcupine and a toad.

When he recovered, Hoggle tried to say something but all that came out was 'Rurpitt, rurpitt.' Each one tried to get back to wizards but they could not so Hairy moved to the woods and Hoggle moved to a pond.

So if you see a toad or porcupine with a sad look in its eye, it may be our friends, Hairy and Hoggle.

Kitty's wobbly tooth

Written and illustrated by Tony Ross

When Kitty's wobbly tooth came out at last, she put it under her pillow, and thought of the 20p she would find in its place in the morning.

'It was only sixpence when I was a lad!' grumbled dad.

'It was only a penny in my day!' pointed out grandad.

Then an idea struck Kitty. If she was to CATCH the tooth fairy, then maybe she could get more than the usual 20p. It was SO obvious, that Kitty couldn't understand why nobody had done it before.

She lay wondering how to do it. 'I'll hold my waste-paper basket over it.' She thought . . . 'No I won't, I don't want to hurt it . . . I know . . .'

Carefully, she set her trap.

Kitty lay awake for hours, imagining pictures in the dark when, all of a sudden, there was a slight movement by her pillow. She lay as still as coal. There was a rustle of paper, the tooth fairy had found the note. (Kitty had written, 'I can't sleep with a great lump of tooth under my pillow. Please look in the dolls' house, you will find it there.')

The fairy's voice was as soft as snow, 'WOW! It must be a big 'un!' she said. Kitty lay still, and she felt, rather than heard, the fairy move from the pillow. Then the lights of the dolls' house went on. (Gran had fixed the lights with a torch battery, some wires, and a little bulb.)

Quick as a blink, Kitty slammed the little door shut.

'GOTCHA!' she cried.

Inside the dolls' house, there was the sound of crashing furniture, and little squeals of anger. When things quietened down, Kitty peeped through one of the tiny windows, and examined her captive.

She had a pretty, though rather cheeky face, with yellow hair all over the place. She wore a wispy white dress, nearly to her toes, and she actually did have . . . coloured WINGS! She really did look exactly like a fairy should look. She didn't sound like one though.

'BATS' DO-DOS!' she yelled, at the huge face looking at her.

'Calling me names will get you nowhere at all' said Kitty calmly, sounding very much like her teacher. 'If you want to get out, then you must pay me a little more for my tooth.'

'More?' gasped the tooth fairy, 'More? How can I give you more? I can only carry one 20p piece at a time. I'm a fairy, in case you haven't noticed, not an elephant. 20p is very heavy!'

Kitty thought about it. The fairy WAS very small.

'In that case,' she said thoughtfully, 'you can stay there till morning, and I'll decide what to do about you. You'll find a little bed upstairs, it may be quite comfy.'

'Hope the bed bugs bite you!' said the fairy crossly.

Although the fairy was trying to be rude, Kitty couldn't help smiling, as she curled up, and went to sleep.

In the morning, there was noise like a moth in a lampshade coming from the dolls' house. The fairy was flinging herself against the door, trying to get out. Kitty put her hand in through the back door, and grasped the fairy's wings firmly. The fairy hit her hard on the fingers with a tiny ironing board that Gran had placed thoughtfully in the tiny kitchen. With a yelp, Kitty pulled her hand away. She put on a winter glove and tried again. This time the fairy tried to bite, but Kitty couldn't feel it through the glove. Quickly, she slipped the fairy into a coffee jar, and screwed down the lid.

'HELP! I'LL SMOTHER!' yelled the fairy, waving her fists.

'No you won't,' replied Kitty, 'I made some holes in the lid.'

Kitty's idea was to be famous. She couldn't remember reading about ANYBODY who had actually caught a fairy. She thought that once the word got around that she had one, then she would get into the papers, then on TV, then maybe her own show, and she would be so rich, she could even afford her own pony. She went downstairs to find Grandad asleep in a chair. She tickled him under the chin, and he opened one eye.

'Do you want to see something FABULOUS!' she said, and held up the jar. The fairy's arms were flat down her side, and her eyes stared straight ahead, as if they were made of glass. Kitty blinked. 'It's not a DOLL,' she said, 'It's a real fairy.' Kitty frowned and rattled the jar, but the fairy didn't twitch a muscle. Then to Kitty's horror, the fairy shouted, 'ALL RIGHT, FATTY, DON'T LOOK!'

Grandad sat up with a jerk.

'You rude, unpleasant girl, he said angrily. 'You'll not come to the library with ME again!' And he stomped off.

'Just then, Gran was coming down the stairs.

'What on EARTH'S all the commotion?' she asked.

'My fairy was rude to Grandad,' Kitty cried, 'Look Gran, a real live fairy. She's a bit naughty though!' So saying, Kitty held up the jar, with the fairy inside, still as stiff as a peg. Gran peered at the fairy. 'I think it's you who's a bit naughty,' she said to Kitty. 'Being rude to your grandad like that, and blaming it on a silly-looking doll.'

When Gran's back was turned, the fairy made a loud, rude noise, 'PPPPPPPrrrrrrrrruuuuurrrppp! Who are you calling silly-looking, Sausage-Legs!'

180

Kitty stiffened, and stared in horror, as Gran turned slowly round.

'You just wait until your mother hears about this,' she said quietly. Gran's angry voice was always quiet. This voice was VERY quiet. Kitty decided not to wait for her mother, and she ran out to play.

Her second-best friend Dominic was getting muddy in the garden next door, when Kitty poked her head through the hedge. She tried to tell him about the fairy. 'GARN!' smirked Dominic, (who most grown-ups thought was awful), 'There ain't no such things as REAL fairies. That one doesn't even LOOK real. It's PLASTIC. I've got a teddy bear that looks more real.'

'And I've seen a monkey's dinner that looks more real than YOU!' screamed the fairy, at the top of her voice.

'Right, Kitty Plunkett . . .' shouted Dominic angrily. He couldn't think of anything else to say, but Kitty knew that she had lost her second-best friend. She also knew that she was not getting very famous.

For the rest of the day, she tried to show people the fairy but always the same thing happened. The fairy stood still as a stone when being looked at, then shouted rude things when no-one was looking. Of course, everybody thought it was just Kitty being horrid.

When Mum and Dad came home, they wouldn't even look at the coffee jar, instead they sent Kitty to bed without a story.

Once in bed, she glared angrily at the fairy, who glared angrily back.

'There's no point HAVING a fairy if no one believes you've got one.' Kitty complained, 'I guess I'll never be famous.'

'You'll never be ANYTHING, kidnapping people, and putting them into jars!' snapped the fairy, 'Remember, it's nice to be important, but it's more important to be nice!'

Kitty unscrewed the lid of the jar.

'You'd better be off, then,' she muttered.

'Help me out then!' snapped the fairy.

'You've got wings, you can fly out.'

'They're not REAL, they are just stitched on to my frock!' grinned the fairy, 'Do you think if I could do magic things, like fly, I'd have spent all day with a great silly lump like you?' Kitty lifted the fairy out of the jar, and put her gently on to the floor.

'If you can't fly, how are you going to get home?' she asked.

'Oh, through cracks and keyholes, little paths and places . . .' and she was gone.

'Hoy! What about this tooth, what about the 20p, IT'S GONE!' yelled Kitty. A little voice came from under the floorboards, 'You can keep the tooth . . . I'll not come again . . .'

And she never did.

Nellie's house

Little Nellie Kettlemould
Lived in a house so very old
The windows creaked and
The carpets curled and
Nellie's ringlets all unfurled;
They stood up straight as pokers —
For a ghost crept, down in the cellar.

Little Nellie Kettlemould
Lived in a house so very cold
The fire froze and
The curtains quivered and
Nellie's bones in her body shivered;
They rattled like dry sticks —
For the ghost crept out of the cellar.

Little Nellie Kettlemould
Lived in a house, but wasn't bold
Enough to run, so
She hid instead
In the darkest place underneath her bed;
The dust went up her nose — atchoo!
And the ghost slipped in and swallowed her.

Little Nellie Kettlemould —
Plays with the ghost in the cellar.

Hugh Scott

I once met a man

I once met a man who said,
'You're looking at someone who's dead!'
'I cried, 'It's not true!'
'I'll prove it to you,'
He smiled as he took off his head.

David Wood

How Ganesh got his elephant head

By Rani Singh

This story is for my two sons, Jairaj and Sukhraj.

Shiva, most powerful god of the Hindus, was married
to a goddess called Parvati.

Parvati always kept a guard at the entrance to her
palace, so she could be sure of privacy and not be
disturbed, especially at bathtime.

'Prepare my bath', Parvati would say, 'Don't forget
to put in milk, honey and almond oil, and make sure it's
just the right temperature.' She then would check that
the guard was at the door, before stepping into her bathing
area. 'Make sure no one enters,' she would say.

Now it so happened, that, one day, Shiva had been
out hunting for deer and was on his way home. He arrived
at the door to his palace. The guard wasn't sure as to what
he should do.

'If I let him in, she'll get annoyed; if I keep him out,
he'll get annoyed. I can't win!' the poor guard thought.

185

Eventually he decided to step aside for the Master of the House and Shiva entered.

Parvati was furious and, that evening, summoned all her girlfriends to her.

'What can I do?' she asked. 'The guards will always obey Shiva before me.'

'Why don't you make your own guard who will just do what you say. You are a goddess and have the gift of life, after all,' said one of the girls.

'Great idea! I'll do it right now!' smiled Parvati. She said a prayer, some magic words, and a cloud of sparkle dust exploded in front of her. When it cleared, there stood the most exquisitely beautiful little boy, strong, handsome with cherry brown eyes, long eyelashes, black hair with golden-brown tints in it, a perfect mouth and a small straight nose. He was dressed in green, with gold jewellery.

'My son!' exclaimed Parvati, 'you will be my special protector.'

'What do you want of me, Mother?' asked the boy, turning his face up towards her. He spoke in a clear, sweet voice, and his laugh was like a tinkling bell.

'Stand guard at my door, and let no one enter', said Parvati, as she went inside, feeling happy and secure at last.

Soon Shiva arrived back at the Palace from his day's hunting. He was surprised to see the boy, and said, 'Stand aside!'

'No! Halt there!' replied the child.

'How dare you! Move out of the way!'

He raised his hand to hit the boy, who managed to duck and level a good karate kick at Lord Shiva.

'Thwack!'

'Foolish! Don't you know who I am?' the God asked.

'No. And you don't know either!' shouted the boy, who jumped and aimed another careful kick.

'Thwack!'

Shiva was so cross at this outrage, that he used his laser vision to stare at the boy who had dared to oppose him. He stared and he stared. He stared so hard that the laser beams from his eyes caused the boy's head to fall off his neck.

'Thud', it went, as it fell on the ground and rolled away. The boy fell down, unconscious.

'What's happened to my son?' cried Parvati, who appeared just at that point, having completed her bath.

'Your son? I didn't have a clue! I'm so sorry,' said Shiva, his face going white as he realized the awfulness of what he'd done. Parvati was in deep distress. She fell back, her eyes closed, into the arms of her servant-girls. She whispered quietly, 'I will wreak death and destruction upon the whole Kingdom if my son is not brought back to life at once,' her eyes still closed.

'Oh dear,' said Shiva. He had to think fast. He summoned his soldiers.

'Go, go to all four corners of the Earth. Search fast, high and low. Bring me back the head of the first creature that you come across.' Shiva turned to his wife.

'It'll be all right dear,' he tried to soothe her. 'I know some magic whereby the boy will be made well again.' Parvati lay silent, still, and angry. The girls fanned her from head to toe, running around, trying to keep her cool.

Eventually a soldier returned — with the head of an elephant.

Shiva looked at the head, then at the boy.

'You fool — it's not' he began, but then he looked at Parvati.

'Oh well, it's better than nothing, I suppose,' he said,

placing the creature's head on the boy's body. The child sat up and looked around, feeling his head with his hands. He looked questioningly at his mother.

Parvati opened her eyes. Everyone held their breath and waited. She looked at the child. Slowly, she smiled.

'My son, I am glad and grateful that you are alive. To me, you look even more beautiful with your elephant head, for you are still mine. I will give you magic, god-like powers and you will be worshipped and praised throughout the world. You will be called Ganesh.'

And so it came to pass. From that day on, before anyone began a new business, took an exam or built a house, it was Ganesh they prayed to for good luck. The boy with the elephant head became one of the most popular gods of the Hindus.

WHEE!

I held my head in both my hands
and flung it through the air.
Borne by the wind it soared away,
streaming out my hair.

The world from high perspectives looked
duller than ditchwater.
I rose above its dreariness —
Halley's comet's daughter.

Higher than the flightpath of dreams,
my cranium sped on.
Whilst, down below, the people said
She's crazy. Head's gone.

It's easy! Just shrug your shoulders,
raise your eyes to the sky.
Then throw your head like a beachball.
Wheee! Goodbye . . . Goodbye . . .

Carol Ann Duffy
Illustrated by Laura Beaumont

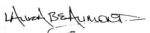

Endpiece

Katie Morag in Hospital.
Mairi Hedderwick.